Kinetics

MultiMind

This is a work of fiction. Names, characters, places, and incidents either are the product of the author's imagination or are used fictitiously. Any resemblance to actual persons, living or dead, events, or locales is entirely coincidental.

Copyright © 2021 by MultiMind

All rights reserved.
No part of this book may be reproduced or used in any manner without written permission of the copyright owner except for the use of quotations in a book review or proper Fair Use.
Fragmented M logo is a trademark of MultiMind Publishing.
For more information, e-mail: multimindpublishing@gmail.com

First paperback edition, September 2022
First e-book edition, September 2022
Audiobook Edition, September 2022

Cover design by Ejiwa Ebenebe

ISBN 978-1-952860-08-9 (paperback)
ISBN 978-1-952860-09-6 (ebook)
ISBN 978-1-952860-21-8 (audiobook)

Library of Congress Control Number: 2022907348

www.multimindpublishing.com

Content Warning:

- Theme of Abuse (Grooming)
- Severe Blood/Violence
- Reference to Sexual Violence

Kinetics

Prologue

The school bell chimed as Latin class started. It was the middle of the day and Ava already wanted to go home. She loathed school, every minute of it. Third class of the day and one more to go. Ava slumped at her second row desk by the stained dry erase board as the remaining students wandered in.

Ava didn't want to check her phone. Nasty messages were already springing up in her notifications by lunch. All created by Roma, all passed around by everyone else. It didn't matter whether or not Ava had classes with Roma or even crossed paths with her that day, Roma always had something awful to say. It has been like this for years, stretching back into middle school. Roma just loved to mess with her for fun – well, Roma liked picking on anyone she could get away with but Ava was a special target for some odd reason. Ava used to wonder why but her curiosity died out long ago. She just wanted to survive the day.

"Everyone, in your seats!" commanded Ms. Dorrell as she leaned back against the front of her wooden desk. She had a shrimp's demeanor: pale pinkish-brown with beady eyes, tall but a bit bent, scuttled a bit as she walked – unless there was a student to harangue. Her hair was short, brown and bobbed, her voice was bored and loud. The chalkboard behind her was filled with streaks from countless washings with dirty water and faint skitters from previous lessons.

The students continued to mill about and chatter until Ms. Dorrell stomped, "*Now!*"

Everyone sat and remained quiet.

"Thank you," the teacher said with strained politeness. She continued in a regular tone, "This is not Freshman year, everyone! You have more to worry about than what is going on in your lives. SATs, ACTs, colleges, the lot. You have to think about your future lives. And there's not a single, decent college that will take a cut-up just because they think they have to. Oh, no. They'll pass you over quick. So please, try to pay attention and let's begin. Starting with the homework from last night, please pass it forward and turn it into the tray."

Ava's body prickled. She didn't get a chance to do it the night before. She was too busy fighting with her mother, Yvonne, over the dishes. Yvonne had found a few dishes sitting in the drying rack that still bore flecks of dried food. When she woke Ava up from napping on the couch, that's when the turmoil began. Yvonne made her do the soiled plates again but Ava's twin brother, Tyrone, pitched in. He dried the dishes and handled the more stubborn stains. This caused more uproar. All the while, their father, Jermaine, reclined in his favorite chair, watching the evening news in his usual sleepy stupor. He never cared to get involved unless forced to.

"Ms. Tanis?" Ms. Dorrell chimed from her desk.

Ava straightened up, alert and afraid.

"Where is your packet? You had all week to finish," the teacher dryly inquired. Students began to giggle but a look from Ms. Dorrell silenced them.

Ava shifted in her seat, her eyes drifted downward. "Um ..., I–"

"Are you answering to the desk or are you answering to me?" Ms. Dorrell snapped.

Jabbed with humiliation, Ava looked up and replied, "I didn't get a chance to finish it–"

"Ms. Tanis, *when* did I give out the assignment?"

Meek as a mouse, Ava replied, "Monday."

"When?" The Latin teacher lifted her sharp chin and gave a disdainful stare down her flat nose.

Louder, Ava repeated, "Mond–"

"'Monday'. Exactly. And what is today?"

"Wednesday." Heat flourished in her chest as her mouth grew dry. All eyes were on her, they pierced like needles.

Ms. Dorrell's voice crawled with bemused surprise, "So that means you had time to work on this. Isn't that right?"

Ava shrugged and sunk her head. The previous night flashed across her mind. Anger bubbled underneath her shame. She wished her mother left her alone; the fighting swallowed up the night. And the night before last was filled with homework from other classes – which she had hardly finished because there was too much of it.

Ms. Dorrell tilted her head as she narrowed her eyes. Her hard-permed bob moved little towards gravity. "Are you telling me you don't know?"

Ava lifted her head and replied, "I had a lot of hom–"

"What college do you plan to go to?"

"I ... I haven't decided ye–"

"'*Not decided*'?" Ms. Dorrell sliced in. "Ms. Tanis, before you know it, it will be Junior year. And then Senior. Besides that, do you think college will have less work or more work?"

Ava mumbled, "More wo–"

"I can't hear you," Ms. Dorrell jabbed.

"More work!" Ava answered. Her blood grew chill with seething. She wanted to bark back at the teacher but it would just cost her more chiding and a quick one-way trip to the administrative office. That's how it always was in that class for others, and she imagined no different for herself.

"Exactly." Ms. Dorrell walked to the window as she rubbed her arms. Her heels clicked behind her words,

"You will not get an easy pass in life, none of you. I didn't tower on the work, I gave a simple packet that should have only taken two nights to do." She hefted open a tall window. A soft, humid summer breeze wafted in. "One night, if you were paying close attention in this class." The teacher sat on the emerald painted sill of the window, "When I give you work to do and set a deadline, I expect that work to be *done* by the deadline. None of this is impossible. Just do the work. Ms. Tanis, you have until tomorrow morning to turn in your packet or your grade on it will drop a whole letter. This means if I don't see that packet in my mailbox by lunch, it will be a B if it was supposed to be an A. If you decide to take more time on it and spend an extra day, it will drop to a C. Spend another day on it and it will be a D – at which point, you might as well not even turn it in. Do I make myself clear?" Ms. Dorrell rubbed her hands. She had a chill that simply wouldn't go away, goosebumps collected on her arms and legs.

"Yes, Ms. Dorrell." Ava replied. She hoped that would be the end.

"Good. You're not going to start this year on the wrong foot." Lifting up from the sill, Ms. Dorrell said, "Now, let's start the class ... is anyone else cold? I guess they turned up the AC too much today. Either way, pull out your books and turn to our last section. We were on section thirteen, page forty-six. Section thirteen, page forty-six."

The rest of the class was fairly normal but Ava kept quiet and small. Every time she wanted to check her phone, she would stop herself mid-grab. Did she really have to see all those terrible messages and tweets just to check the time? Ava's Twip account was the worst of them all. Every new notification was an insult or jeer. She found it pointless to even try visiting the app or use it. Ava used to be invited to so many TwipGroup chatrooms, she had to turn off the invitation feature. Every chat was the same: she would be invited again and again, and if she accepted, the chat would just be full of abuse towards her. If she didn't, the invitations would just continue. Endlessly. If she blocked one person, another would invite her.

But she looked at her phone anyway. She had to – there was a text from her mother layered atop the Twip notifications. Ava looked for Ms. Dorrell. She was in the back of the classroom helping a struggling student by lambasting their intelligence. Ava nestled her phone in her lap, tapped the text message notification and opened her phone.

> **Mom**: Dn't fgt to do ALL chores
> **Mom**: Ty cn't help
> **Mom**: No napping

This incensed Ava. Before she could reply, another tweet rolled in. It was a meme of her eating in the school cafeteria with a horse's head instead. As with most of the terrible tweets, it came from an anonymous account. Ava used to show them to the teachers and administrators but their half-hearted attempts to find the culprits dissuaded her from even trying any further. She could tell it was

Roma's work because the memes would gravitate around whatever she had said to Ava personally. But every time an administrator or teacher would ask Roma if she made those tweets or said those terrible things, Roma would play innocent and say it wasn't her. "They certainly aren't from my account," was her alibi. "I don't know why Ava blames me so much. She's so obsessed with me."

The torment tapered off just before the summer started after her brother intervened. To this day, Ava didn't know what he did but whatever it was, it made Roma and her associates keep their distance. Or at least, keep the harassment online. There were still whispers around the school but at least most of them ceased when Ava was around. She still wasn't sure if that was a good thing or a bad thing – but at least things were quiet offline.

Ms. Dorrell's heels clicked their way towards the front. Ava rushed into her phone settings to turn off all her notifications and thrusted the phone under her leg. Hearing how close the clicks were, Ava was sure Ms. Dorrell had seen her. Anxiety flared within her chest – Ms. Dorrell loved to take away phones and turn them over to administrators. Several students had already learned this first hand and the year had just begun. But Ms. Dorrell breezed past as if Ava wasn't there. Not even a dismissive glance. She even grew an extra scuttle in her step.

The class bell rang and Ava gathered up her things. Nestling in the last book, she zipped up her mesh aqua backpack and shuffled out the room. Ava passed a small cluster of students.

One snickered, "There goes horse–"

"Shut uuuuup!" another hissed. "Her brother is *super* crazy."

Ava walked away faster; she didn't want to hear any more. Tyrone never told her what he did to Roma or if he ever suffered being picked on but from the glimmer of comments, she was certain he was. It didn't help that she knew he loved all things esoteric and occult. If it was unusual, he gravitated towards it. And he didn't do much to hide it. That certainly had to earn him some ridicule.

Ava kept her head down as she stormed to the next class, Biology. Another class whose homework she hadn't completed. She weaved through the other students in the crowded hall, both hands clutched on the single strap draped over her shoulder. This was her everyday: stay small as possible, become as little of a target as possible. Her phone sat quiet in her pocket but she knew it was filling up with new obscenities. The torrents were always the worst between classes.

She pattered down the school stairwell and walked into class. Biology was a bit more relaxed than Latin but not by much. Mr. Farrowat was a stocky man with a bushy mustache who graduated university with honors but somehow decided to become a high school biology teacher. "I want to give back," he would express at the start of every year. No one could believe him.

"In your seats, everyone!" He called out as he readied his school-marked laptop on his desk in front of the whiteboard. "C'mon, class is going to start as soon as the bell rings so get ready!"

Some students obeyed and slid into their seats, others stayed where they were. Ava sat at a lonely side table close to the door, head down. *Someone's gonna take a picture of this*, fleeted across her mind but she lost the will to care. Everything she did garnered ridicule.

Few students sat with her. The seats and red lacquered tables were assigned but Ava's table became a bit scarce after a shouting match she had with another student. They kept mocking her voice and ribbed for others to join in. The growing crowd kept asking her questions about horses and the validity of Roma's statement that Ava was dating her twin brother. To simmer the heat, Mr. Farrowat re-did the seating chart and only placed the quiet and studious at her table. He felt proud, she felt singled out.

Ava rummaged through her backpack to collect her books. A light chill brimmed inside her mesh bookbag. She ignored it, it was just something that happened every once in a while. She picked out her cherry-covered binder and waited for the class to start with her head slumped on her arms.

One person zipped in right before the bell chime, and Ava was glad to see her. Her best friend, Lexi. Dolled up as always, almost late as always. They exchanged quick hellos as Lexi hurried to her seat at the back of the room. Harsh scrapes of chairs against the wax floor filled the room as Mr. Farrowat closed his laptop.

"First things first!" The teacher announced. "Send in

your homework! Send your homework in! Homework for the questions in chapter three, section two in your book." A student halfway in the back raised his eager hand. "Yes, Darnell?"

"This was too hard!" The pin-thin boy lamented. "I hardly understood anything! Can you go easy since it's the start of the school year? Y'know, 'learnin' curve' an' all?"

The rest of the class agreed as they pooled their scribbled pages of notebook paper at the center of their table. The three other students at Ava's table had their pile ready as soon as Mr. Farrowat spoke.

The biology teacher rolled his grey eyes and sighed, "Darnell, we went over this in *class*. If you were paying attention – if any of you were paying attention – then this assignment wouldn't be so hard." He began to walk about to each table to collect the stacks as he continued, "This isn't the Honors track, everyone! You all have little to complain about, I made sure that the questions were easy. Even a half-asleep kid could have googled this and passed. Maybe if you spent less time on Twip – this includes *you* Marcus, put the phone away or I will take it – or at least more *constructive* time on TwipSearch, this wouldn't seem so hard. I didn't have these things when I was your age. All we had were encyclopedias and sometimes they were outdated. Twip, Google, whatever, it's all at your fingertips now."

When Mr. Farrowat came to collect the pile of homework at Ava's table, he noticed it was one short. "Ava," he said quietly, "where is your homework? This is the third time already, you're not getting off to a good start."

A mischievous student overheard and commented, "Her brother–"

"Dorian, one more word and it's the Administrator's office for you," Mr. Farrowat threatened. He turned on a heel to the joking boy and reminded, "I'm still astonished that you're still here, given your behavior as a freshman. Does your *father* need to come up here or your *mother*? They seemed to be incredibly *eager* in your improvement. Your father was like the Flash the last time and your mother doesn't work that far away."

Dorian quieted as classmates snickered. "I'll – I'll shut up," he mumbled to himself and looked away.

Mr. Farrowat turned back to Ava, "Get this in *tomorrow*. All of it. I don't care what you have to do, just do it, okay? You're a smart girl, I want you to show that off."

Ava sank in her seat, "Okay." A small surge of irritation erupted within her again. She had no idea how she was going to finish tonight's assignments and the back-pile. She sulked in her seat.

The biology teacher sauntered off to collect more papers. The other students looked away before Ava could meet their eyes. She was certain they were judging her.

Class was long and tedious, seconds dragged like hours. Angered by her circumstances, Ava wanted to be left alone. She wanted to snap at anyone, everyone. The fact that Mr. Farrowat kept calling on her so many times didn't help. She wanted to bark at him to stop.

At one point during class, a girl with blue box braids and glossy cherry lips huddled herself next to Ava's chair as Mr. Farrowat marked evolution theories on the whiteboard. Her sudden arrival startled Ava on the inside but she dared not show it. The girl had a Cheshire smile as she whispered eagerly, "'Ey, Marrisa been sayin' things about you. Your brother gonna take care of her, too?"

The table behind Ava broke into a fit of light laughter. Ava's stomach sank from the attention.

"I don't care, okay? Go away, Penelope," Ava brushed off. She tried to return her attention to the whiteboard but Penelope kept talking.

"You don't care?" she tittered. Penelope threw a hand over her mouth as she checked back at the chuckling table. "You know Roma and Marissa *always* be talkin' 'bout you, right? What? Alexandria taught you some kung fu moves from her dad? Or is your brother gonna do somet–"

"Penelope!" Mr. Farrowat clapped. The student was caught off-guard by the sudden baritone of his voice. "What are you *doing*?"

Her smile unmoved, Penelope stood up and answered, "I was just askin' Ava for somethin'. Like, a pad or tampon or whatever."

The class erupted with a mixture of disgust and laughter. Ava closed her eyes and felt tears begin to sear, she felt so humiliated and dragged along. She didn't want to be caught misty-eyed. The last Ava wanted was the class to think she was crying.

Mr. Farrowat wasn't impressed. "Penelope, if you need

those things, wouldn't you think the *nurse* would be a better choice rather than bother your own classmates? Go to the nurse."

Penelope shook her head, "Nah, I think I'm good–"

"Go to the nurse or get written up," Mr. Farrowat demanded.

Penelope was taken aback, "Get written up for what? I wasn't doin' anything!"

"For disrupting class–"

"I wasn't disruptin' nothin'! I was quiet!" she defied. "You ain't hear me–"

"Nurse or administrator's office. Your choice, not mine," Mr. Farrowat stated. The class was silent.

Penelope stood there for a moment, baffled. Then she sucked her teeth and stormed out of the classroom.

Mr. Farrowat took a deep breath to steady himself. He spoke to the rest of the class, "Like I said before all this commotion, there are various biomes that affect evolution...."

Ava sank her head down onto her arms. She kept her eyes low, she could feel tears gathering and wanted no one to see. This was her every day. Her every single day.

Chapter 1

The sun basked down as Ava sat on the bus bench. She avoided the broken slats and tried to not mind the wobbly cement base. She messed with the notification settings on her phone. She wanted digital solace but she still wanted updates from XinBō.

The app opened up when she okayed the new settings. It was a wave of sea colors that opened to where she left off, her journal. She typed a new entry:

Sept 23, 2015

Mood: Exhausted

My brother always loved me and I'm grateful for it.

> Another awful day. Everyone is on my *case*! Forget my homework for a couple classes and everybody goes crazy! No slack, no nothin! They all get on my nerves!
>
> Ma then trippin over the fact I ain't clean the dishes right because I rushed thru em. Dad's just sayin nothin like always do. Like he not even there!
>
> Ty's the *only* one lookin out for me. The *only* one. I don't know if it's twin-connection or something but he always is there for me. Never got on my case unless it's serious, actually *tries* to help me out. He don't dog me for stupid reasons or *nothin*. I wish it was only us sometimes.

Ava Tanis posted the update as "Private". An animated gray eye blinked on her screen in confirmation. She wanted to check her other notifications but she already had a good idea what was there. Ava checked the time and looked up at the schedule posted on the bus stop. The bus was late *again*. Late and probably *very* crowded with rowdy students. *Prolly be faster if I just walked*, Ava thought as she leaned over to check the street. No bus in sight. She sat back, blowing out a derisive breath, and decided to give the bus a bit more time. Ava didn't feel like standing on a crowded bus but she didn't feel like walking the half hour it would take on foot, either.

She slipped her phone into her back pocket as she fumed about her day. Ava couldn't wait for the day to be over. The school year had only just started and already teachers were giving her grief. Every other elder in her life was the same: Telling her what she *should* do, what she *shouldn't* do, what job she *should* get, what job she *shouldn't* get, what college she *should* go to, what college she *shouldn't* go to, who she *should* be, who she *shouldn't* be. The same nag, the same rag.

Over the hill far away, the 23 bus sat at a red light. Through the dark tinted windows, Ava saw there weren't many people. It must have been a lagging bus. No matter, a lagging bus with plenty of seats was much better than a crowded bus or no bus at all. *The only good thing to happen to me today*, Ava mused as she gathered her things.

As the red and yellow bus headed down the hill, Ava fished out her monthly student pass from the messy front pocket of her backpack. She had the same card since she started Melissa Elliot High School, the plastic neon yellow card was bent and faded. Then the bus arrived. Its gears whined to a stop and the doors hissed open as it idled with the rumble of a neglected diesel truck engine. The cool, stale air greeted Ava as she stepped aboard and swiped her card. There were plenty of seats to choose from, as the bus was near vacant and had more adults than students. She plunked down in a seat behind the driver. The driver grunted the next stop and shut the door. He was a portly, languished man just as intent on going home as she was.

Bookbag on her lap, Ava pulled back out her phone

and unlocked it. She learned about XinBō from Lexi a couple years ago and had been using it ever since. The fact it was only popular on the other side of the planet was her favorite feature. Her own little special corner of the internet. Away from the bullies, away from the drama and nonsense. On XinBō, Ava could be herself. The people were different. The topics were different. Everything was different. More vibrant.

She would post updates about her life, play time-killers, dress up her avatar, Wix23, or mind the small house it lived in. Her avatar was a stubby, bubble-faced, cherry-lipped glam girl with deep brown skin and silver bobbed hair. Whenever Ava was bored, she would send her avatar into the diamond portal outside its house to visit chatrooms. Like now.

Tapping the glowing wormhole diamond, Wix23 walked to her doorstep on her tiny, heeled feet. The bus rumbled past an empty stop. The screen turned silver as it loaded possible chatrooms. A single, small diamond appeared and spun fast or slow as new worlds loaded. Deals and tips on how to navigate the chatrooms and games popped up underneath the rotating diamond.

Moments later, a miniature city appeared on the screen. Each location designated a different chatroom. There was a party house, decked out in fall colors to mark the passing of the seasons; a beach with rippling waves and small fishermen posed on a dock; a park that featured turning leaves; and a city center that mimicked a jumble between Hollywood and Times Square. A golden statue billboard covered in blinking lights spelled out "XinBō Centre".

Given that the digital city loaded in a couple minutes, Ava guessed there weren't a lot of people on. *Most of the users are probably sleep right now*, she figured as the bus idled at another stop light. A passenger chimed the yellow tape along the walls for the next stop, it rang with a metallic ding. Three more stops to go for Ava and they were going along quicker than expected.

Before Ava could pick any of the chatrooms, a bar notification appeared and a doorbell popped up on her app's screen. Both read: Ra1nwater is visiting! Go now?

Ava tapped the doorbell with her thumb. The diamond loading screen popped back up. She looked up and saw her stop approaching, she readied her bag as the bus churned its way down Sandoval Ave. The bus stop was empty and decrepit, the bench was in crumbles and splinters, dandelions sprouted everywhere. The flowers were dotted along the vacant lot behind the stop.

Checking her phone, Ava dinged for her stop. The avatar was home again, bobbling and teetering about. The home had a summer flare. Ocean sand slushed in a corner around a shell-shaped hot tub, fishing nets graced the mint stripe walls with scattered pearls. The lamp hanging over the door was a beach ball. Under it stood an avatar wearing a pastel shark kigurumi on a golden welcome rug.

The bus squealed to a stop in front of the shattered bench, and Ava slumped her bag onto her shoulder and gripped the rail to stand. She could feel the rumble through the silver railing and her feet. Ava's phone chirped as she trotted down the triplet of stairs. The bus driver grunted out the next station and pulled the double doors shut. The bus drove off with a belch of black smoke. Ava checked her phone, but the afternoon sun behind her made it hard to see. After she fumbled with the brightness on her dark screen, Ava saw a tiny speech bubble float above Ra1nwater's head: Hi!

In the chat box on the lower half of the screen, an amber speech bubble pointing left appeared: Ra1nwater shared a greeting!

Ava started walking past the stop to cross the wide, abandoned parking lot. Echoes of a small convenience store remained, broken off walls of brick and busted windows covered in errant sprawls of dandelions and blossoms. The markings for the parking lot were still untouched, blow flowers swayed in the cracks as Ava stepped past in her dingy white sneakers.

She selected a wave greeting from the selection scrolled under the text box. Ava didn't want to be too distracted while crossing this lot; she had heard stories of jumpings on the less-than-aware and she didn't want to be preyed on by surprise. She kept her head up and alert as she made her way along. Her home sat on the other side, a red rowhouse with a few sunflowers sprouting in front of the raised stone porch.

Almost at the other end of the lot, Ava heard another chirp. She checked her phone.

> **Ra1nwater**: How ya doin?
> **Ra1nwater**: You looked pissed in bio

Ava looked about and then tapped out a quick response:

> **Wix23**: So much bull today. All of it

Ava stepped onto the cracked, jaunted sidewalk and crossed the pockmarked street to the cement stairs that led to the cherrywood door of 12 Docker Ave. The black mailbox by the door hung open, Ava tapped it closed. As she fished for her keys, she read the response she just received.

> **Ra1nwater**: What happened?
> **Ra1nwater**: School just started
> **Ra1nwater**: Is Roma messing with yoi
> **Ra1nwater**: *you?

The front door swung open with quick creaks. It was her twin brother, Tyrone, in a blue polo and denim pants. Like Ava, he had a medium build and lanky stature. It always baffled her how the both of them were let out at the same time but he always made it home before her.

"You're just getting home now?" Ty joked. He stepped through the threshold in his grey socks to slip Ava's bookbag off her shoulder with care and invite her in warmly. Ava padded through with a shy smile. Though she appreciated her doting brother, sometimes he doted too much. But she would remind herself: enjoy it now, he won't always be there to shoulder her burdens. College was only two years away.

"Ty," Ava smiled, "I had it, y'know." Her phone chirped.

Tyrone closed the door as he eyed his sister with a cocked eyebrow and a defiant smirk.

"What? I can't help out my baby sister?" He hefted Ava's bookbag onto his shoulder and followed her around the round pillar that separated the doorway and the living room to the chocolate couch. The living room was spacious and simple, with tan carpet stairs in front of the door and an entertainment center nestled against the wall between the kitchen and dining room. Warm and homely.

Ava chuckled, "We were born at the same time!" Standing in the living room, illuminated by the open windows and thick curtains pulled tightly aside, Ava checked her phone and typed a quick reply:

> **Wix23**: Not her. Other stuff. Home w Ty.
> brb

"Who you talkin' to?" Tyrone inquired as he sat Ava's bookbag beside the aged microfiber couch. Some of the pillows were mismatched from couches past. Tyrone's black tablet was nestled between a peach polka dotted pillow and a smooth brown one. The television played in silence, a home shopping channel.

Ava pocketed her phone, "Lexi. She saw I was irritated today and wanted to check up on me."

The phone chirped again.

Tyrone held out his arms as he made his way to his sister, scoffing, "Whatever. Lay it on me, your big brother."

He wrapped his arms around her and slid his hands down her arms to guide her to the couch. Ava chuckled again and tried to correct him but it fell on deaf ears. She snuggled up beside him. Tyrone laid his head atop hers, his cheek shifting a long braid or two around her crown. He smelled of spice while she smelled of cherries. They suited each other well.

"Baby sis," Tyrone reminded gently, "I was born two hours before you. That makes you my baby sis. Now, what happened?" He laced a hand over her tilted hip.

Ava sighed and shifted her head better on Tyrone's shoulder. She cushioned her cheek against his muscle, what little of it he had. She always felt safe and protected like this, deep in her brother's arms, hearing his deepening voice, hearing his pulse. Nothing could touch her, nothing could harm her. She needed his comfort, she knew that.

"Everything."

"'Everything'?" her brother echoed. "Like what? That Roma girl buggin' you again?" Ava could feel Tyrone's shoulder tense.

"Nah, nah. It's Ms. Dorrell. She got on my case about forgetting my homework in front of the class. Mr. Farrowat in Bio got upset too but didn't go into a whole lecture about it like Ms. Dorrell did. And not in front of the whole class, neither!"

Tyrone eased some. "Oh, ok. I was about to say, 'I thought I handled that.' Thought she was getting out of pocket again. Sounds like I'mma have to handle *this* problem a little later. Haven't you had Ms. Dorrell before or was that somebody different?"

"Somebody different," Ava confirmed. Almost every teacher Ava had was tough on her. The school figured it was the best way to prepare their students for the "real world".

"Ok. The school year just started, though," Tyrone commiserated. "Why she buggin' out 'bout it now?"

Ava sighed angrily. "She wanted to go on and on about how I'm starting the year on the wrong foot and how it's gonna affect my life and career and how I need to start thinking about how colleges will see me and stuff."

Tyrone sucked his teeth. "Not even five full weeks into school and she's already tryna act like you're about to flunk out!"

"I know, right?" Ava vented, bolting upright. Tyrone lulled her back to his shoulder and petted her head, smoothing her edges.

"She needs to stay in her lane," Tyrone seethed. The air grew a little thick.

Ava ears perked. He was falling into a mood again, she could tell. She tried to soothe him, "But it's not that big of a deal, though!" Ava didn't want her brother to fix her dilemmas, he was the ... heavy-handed type, out of passion. He never struck her or anyone she saw but she always felt *something* happens when Tyrone gets involved.

Once, there was a boy in her neighborhood that would catcall her at every chance and opportunity. Tyrone caught wind of it and the boy wound up in the hospital. The boy said Tyrone did it but Tyrone said when he went over to talk to the boy, he found the child bashing his own head in on the jagged stone wall outside his house. No outside force, no nothing, all doctor reviews pointed to self-inflicted wounds. But Ava felt something was amiss.

Then there was Roma. Once Tyrone promised he would step in, that's when the "crazy brother" rumors started. To this day, he never told her what he did. Tyrone only assured her that Roma would keep her distance.

As Ava continued to try to simmer her brother's temper, her phone vibrated and sung out a crescendo of chirping birds. Tyrone looked down at his sister as she pulled out her phone and saw "Lexi" beaming.

Ava tried to get up, "Gotta take this."

Tyrone clutched her hips and brought her back beside him, "Why can't you take it here?"

Ava glanced at her brother with masked unease and took the call.

"Hey, Lexi," Ava greeted with a false calm.

"Hey!" A charismatic voice greeted back. "Still with Ty or can we talk?"

Tyrone interjected, overhearing the call, "Y'all can still talk around me." Ava cringed, Tyrone slipped a hand over her waist.

A couple beats of silence and Lexi continued, unsure,

"Oh – okay. Uh, Ava ... what's up? I ain't hear much from you. You ok?"

Ava replied, "Yeah, yeah. I'm fine. Just Ms. Dorrell got on me today." She looked up at her brother, who lightly thumbed her waist and draped an arm around her shoulders. He met her gray eyes and tapped his forehead to hers lovingly. Ava smiled at her brother, "Ty helped me through it."

Lexi knew of Tyrone's ways, but she tried to push past it, "Well, if you're doin' oka–"

"She's just fine, Lexi," Tyrone affirmed flatly. Ava knew he wasn't irritated ... but he was getting there.

Tyrone nuzzled Ava's ear. She thought he was doting over her but he whispered, "Will she be talking like this forever?"

Ava tensed up, her voice quickened, "Uh, Lexi ... since that's over, anything else you wanna talk about?"

Lexi caught on. "Nah, not really. I just wanted to see how you were doing but if you're doing okay, I'll see you online later."

Ava nodded, "Hm, okay! I'll catch up with you later! Bye, Lex–"

"Byeeeeeee, *Lexi*," Tyrone feigned sweetly.

Lexi hung up and Ava's phone turned dark. Ava laid her phone down in her lap and gazed up at her brother.

With a heavy sigh, Tyrone reached over to the glass top coffee table in front of them and grabbed the TV remote. His resting hand traced across Ava's shoulders and down her bare arm as he reached and traced its way back up to its resting place as he sat back. The air in the room leavened some.

"Let's watch some TV, okay?" Tyrone suggested.

Ava nodded and laid her head back on his shoulder as Tyrone turned up the TV and sorted through the channels. Tyrone snickered to himself, flipping along, "I can't believe I picked up the remote to do this. I should be able to turn the TV on by myself by now."

"Hm?" Ava looked up at her twin. His angular jaw still bore no scruff or whiskers. His hair was thick and braided into swirls, a feat carried out by a visiting aunt a couple weeks ago. Otherwise, his hair would be out and wild. The aunt was so deeply frustrated by Tyrone's silence and one-word answers to every question she asked. By the time the aunt left, she chalked it up to being a teenage boy and dropped the issue.

"I'm still learning," Tyrone continued. "Don't want to blow up anything unless I absolutely have to." He snickered to himself at the thought. He settled on a different home-shopping channel, where a hyper announcer sold floral dish sets. He laid down the remote and picked up Ava's hand. He rubbed her fingertips with his thumb and examined them.

"Have *you* been doing anything?" Tyrone asked. The television volume lowered by itself.

Ava watched him rub her fingertips like a coin. She shook her head. "Nah, I haven't. Not really."

Tyrone sighed again, exasperated. He pulled her hand to his heart, still rubbing her fingertips. He chided to her with a tired face, "You gotta *practice*, baby sis. How can we get strong together if you don't practice?"

Ava tried to humor him, "I ... uh ... I'm not as good at it as you." A shy smile curled upon her face.

Tyrone was unmoved.

"Ava," his voice was stern and dry, "whatever shall I do with you, baby sister?" He drew her fingertips to his face and gave them a soft kiss. Ava felt a small spark. "Please don't let your big brother down. I love you too much for that." He looked her in the eyes, "Promise?"

Ava was held by his stare. "I promise."

"Good," Tyrone sat back, satisfied. He saw the time on the shopping ticker at the bottom of the TV: 4:56 PM.

He patted Ava on the shoulder, "You need to do your homework before Ma and Dad come home. Go do that. I'll be wherever you need me."

Ava slipped her hand away to pick up her phone and got up. She hooked her bookbag and slumped it over her shoulder on her way to the stairs. Tyrone watched her diligently as he leaned over to grab his tablet and wake it up.

Seeing the upstairs light turn on and the last of her shadow leave, Tyrone returned his focus to the television. The hyper presenter was selling blankets now. Annoyed and bored, Tyrone rolled his eyes and blinked them. The channel changed to a random action movie more than halfway over. He propped up a leg on the coffee table and started scrolling through his tablet.

Upstairs, Ava sat on her bed with her lavender door closed and her unopened bookbag slumped against her legs. Her room was small, just like Tyrone's, which was further down the hall on the other side. Unlike Tyrone's, her room was decorated with whimsy and color. She had a giant ice cream cone lamp on her purple dresser, a recent birthday gift from Lexi. Loose jewelry scattered about the base of the lamp, some pieces she hadn't worn for years. More forgotten pieces of jewelry collected in the join between the dresser and the floor. Her walls were robin egg blue, complete with the speckles. She still remembered how her father and brother spent all weekend on those speckles, mostly arguing over every placement. That was three years ago, and she still loved them. A squat, sparse-filled bookcase sat next to her dresser filled with piles of comic books and random figurines. Beside her bookcase was her closed closet, small and packed tight across from her bed. Her bed had a brilliant firework-covered summer comforter and lined sparrows on her sheets. Ava got comfortable on her bed and opened her phone to XinBō.

Win23 was alone in the house, striking various poses or looking around. Dusk began to fall outside the avatar's windows. Ava tapped the golden telephone in the corner of the room and her friend's list popped up. The list was short, mainly people Ava had a couple good conversations with, but never heard from again after accepting their friend request. However, they had interesting feeds so Ava kept them anyways.

It was a short scroll to Ra1nwater's name, Ava tapped the house icon beside it. There was a green dot hanging in the corner of the house, she was available. The diamond loading screen appeared and a moment later, Wix23 was in a cluttered house filled with knick knacks from rare gachas and contests, two baths, a large heart shaped canopy bed, and a crystal purple birdcage rocking next to her golden telephone.

Ava typed:

>**Wix23**: You there? I'm by myself now

It took a couple minutes but Ra1nwater appeared in her shark kigurumi. Jumping excitedly, Ra1nwater said:

>**Ra1nwater**: Yay! Yu haz freedumz!

Ava rolled her eyes with a smirk and replied:

>**Wix23**: You know how big brothers are
>**Wix23**: *how brothers are

Ra1nwater gave a concerned reaction.

>**Ra1nwater**: Dat bugs me a lil
>**Ra1nwater**: He's your *twin* brother

> **Ra1nwater**: I know he was born first
> but he's still your *twin*
> And he needs to let you do
> things on your own
>
> **Ra1nwater**: You ain't six
>
> **Wix23**: I know, I know
>
> **Wix23**: He just wanna keep me safe

Ra1nwater switched from a shark kigu to a punk school girl outfit with a silver-white beehive hairdo. It complimented her brown skin and glossy peach lips. She then facepalmed.

> **Ra1nwater**: He wanna keep you to
> himself
>
> **Ra1nwater**: He know y'all not datin,
> right?

Ra1nwater threw her head back in a belly laugh. Wix23 shot a look of irritation.

> **Wix23**: That's not funny
>
> **Wix23**: You're an only child, you don't
> get it
>
> **Ra1nwater**: Do you *seriously* think
> all siblings r lik this?
>
> **Ra1nwater**: srsly?

Ava sighed out loud.

> **Wix23**: You don't get it!
> **Ra1nwater**: He's gonna kill your first boyfriend
> **Ra1nwater**: You know that right?
> **Wix23**: Stop messing about, Lexi

Ra1nwater folded her arms and gave out an animated huff.

> **Ra1nwater**: Fiiiiiiiiiiiine. I just don't like him not leeting you be inpedent
> **Ra1nwater**: *Letting
> **Ra1nwater**: *Indepentdent.
> **Ra1nwater**: All my English is *gone* today
> **Wix23**: He's just a bit over protective.
> **Wix23**: Can we talk about something else?

A few moments passed. Both avatars started striking random poses and looking about.

> **Ra1nwater:** Are you *sure* you don't want to talk about Ms. Dorrell?

Wix23 shook her head no.

> **Wix23**: Can we talk about *anything* else?
> **Wix23**: Liiiike, how was *your* day?

There was another pause. Ava was about to type something but Ra1nwater replied.

> **Ra1nwater**: Nothing new. Dad making adobo tonite
> **Ra1nwater**: Adobo and greens for dindin
> **Ra1nwater**: #BlasianLiving

Wix23 smiled and laughed.

> **Wix23**: Don't he like nvr make that unless somethin special happens?
> **Ra1nwater**: Or ma bug him just because
> **Ra1nwater**: Either Imma get surprised with something or hes just being watever

Two quick double knocks rapped against Ava's door, it was Tyrone.

> **Wix23**: BRB

Ava placed her phone on silent and darkened it before she wedged it under her lap. Tyrone peered in and noticed the unopened backpack and the corner of her phone poking out. "You haven't started yet?" he asked.

Ava immediately zipped open her bookbag and pulled out all the contents all over her bed. "I wanted to relax a bit and catch up on what I missed on the internet today," she hurried out as she flapped open her binder. "I'm gettin' on it now, bro."

Chapter 2

Dinner at the Tanis residence was uneventful that night. Though there was a large and luxurious wood dining table, the family rarely ate there. That's where all the bills lived. Instead, everyone ate in the living room around the television. An old technicolor Western played on the dingy flatscreen TV, picked by Jermaine. He sat on the couch next to his wife, the both of them balancing a glass plate of steamed tilapia and vegetables on their laps.

Jermaine was round and worn from the years spent in warehouses and manufacturing. He rose from item packer to a department manager in twenty years. Yvonne used to be slimmer in her younger years but pregnancy and working as a loan officer at the local bank added to her figure. Both Jermaine and Yvonne used to be athletic and active together, it was how they met, but time has calmed them into the comfortable rut they were grounded in. Away from them, Tyrone sat on the floor in front of the coffee table, his orange plate beside him. His picked apart slab of fish grew cold, his tablet nestled in his lap with a dim glow.

Away in her room, Ava worked slavishly through the back-pile. Yvonne had brought her plate up earlier, the red platter sat atop her closed math textbook, empty. Wanting a break, Ava set aside her Bio homework and got up to stretch and change into her bed clothes. She slipped on a faded red, oversized shirt and drew up her braids into a messy, loose top bun. Ava plopped herself back down on the bed and fished out her phone. She reasoned to herself that she already completed Math II and Art History so she should be allowed a short break.

Ava visited her social feeds to clear the number bubble resting at the corner of each app. She knew she wouldn't find anything substantial, she just wanted to clear the numbers. Ava then opened XinBō to catch up on her webcomics, scroll through the fashion snaps and skim her feed. Ava couldn't read most of the captions but she always told herself she'd one day pick up Mandarin. Despite the language barrier, the pictures she saw were stunning, a viewport into a better, prettier world. When it came to her webcomics, she followed translation accounts for fan scans. Ava had Lexi to thank for that. Lexi herself could barely piece together the Chinese, Tagalog was her better second tongue.

Updated and satisfied, Ava went to her avatar's house and tapped on her daily diamond claim, displayed by a glowing diamond rotating in the bottom corner of her screen. She already had three hundred and twenty-eight in two days because she rarely spent them on in-app apparel and games. Lexi, on the other hand, always spent her diamonds on anything that remotely caught her fancy – which was nearly *everything*.

Wix23 tried to visit Ra1nwater's house but an away message popped up:

> **Ra1nwater isn't home right now!
> Leave a message?**

Ava figured it was probably the universe telling her to finish her homework. She pulled back open her Bio work and started on the next problem.

The clock turned and turned but still Ava wasn't done. It was almost half past midnight and everyone else had already gone to bed. Only Tyrone stopped in an hour ago to kiss her goodnight on her forehead, just like every night. Even when Ava spent the night away from home, Tyrone sent a text that just had a kiss and a black girl emoji. She had finished Bio but was only a third through her Latin homework packet. Ava yawned wide. Her bundled braids lolled in the general direction of her every head tilt.

She didn't want to fall asleep but she kept drifting, slipping off. Her head kept nodding and, once, she could have sworn the pen she dropped slid back into her hand by itself. Completely defeated, Ava shoved away her schoolwork and laid out on the bed. The overhead light went off and her covers drew over her.

Morning came. The peeking sun and singing birds woke Ava with a start. Latin still wasn't done. And she still hadn't touched any of her current homework. Ava stared at the thinning oak tree outside her window as her foggy brain tried to spin the math. The only sum it could establish was that "sun" equals "not enough time/too late".

Ava checked her phone: 6:15 AM. Forty-five minutes before she had to get up for school. As the clouds of dusk sailed away, Ava picked up her pen and furiously tried to complete the rest of her homework.

By the time the alarm beeped, Ava was only halfway through the rest of her Latin packet. She was screwed and she knew it, the alarm only confirmed by how much.

Guess I'm just gonna hafta turn this in and beg for some mercy, Ava sulked in defeat as she slid off her bed and checked her phone. Latin was third period but she knew much better than to try to finish her work in Art II beforehand. Ms. Farrah would just make another example out of her. She even once made another student cry because she kept saying, "STEM kids – if they're so smart, why can't this one stop dropping their pastel chalk? Will you build a robot to clean up your mess as I wait or do you not care about this class at all because no numbers are involved? I teach students, not calculators. Maybe you don't need school since you're so brilliant." Ava would rather keep her head down and hope for invisibility. And figure out how to do the regular History homework on her phone at lunch time, for it had completely slipped her mind – up until now.

Two quick double knocks rapped at her door and Tyrone entered, before Ava could utter a word or move. A navy robe hung heavy off his shoulders, covering his tank top and basketball shorts. He always rose before her and was always the first person she saw.

"Mornin', baby sister," he greeted softly.

Ava smiled with fatigue.

Tyrone frowned, "What's wrong?" He outstretched his arms. A stroke of sunlight lit the room a little brighter.

Ava clambered up off the bed and wrapped herself around her brother. His robe smelled of cinnamon and hickory. She tucked her chin over his shoulder and said, "Nothing. Just ... homework tired me out. I got enough of it done, though."

"'Enough'?" Tyrone repeated with suspicion. He lassoed her small frame a little tighter.

When Ava pulled away from the embrace, she felt resistance. The guilt of not finishing panged at her. She looked her brother in the eyes, his hands resting on her waist. He knew her and knew her well. He just wanted the best for her. Didn't all big brothers?

She brought herself close once more, rested her head on Tyrone's shoulder, and his arms enveloped her again.

"I'm fine, Ty," Ava tried to reassure. "It's just homework."

Tyrone rubbed her back warmly. "Hmmmm," he mused aloud. He wasn't convinced, Ava could tell.

She pulled herself away again, the break caused a slightly tighter resistance, and pecked her brother on the cheek. Her go-to for leniency and mercy.

"I'mma go brush my teeth," she said. "I'm tellin' you, Ty, I got this. I'm fine." She slipped past her brother and left her room.

As she walked down the stubby hall to the open, dark bathroom at the end, Ava heard Tyrone close her door as he left her room and pad down the stairs. The hall itself barely had any light, both Tyrone's and their parents' doors were closed. Ava drifted out a light sigh, *Ty worries too much sometimes*. She entered the bathroom.

Ava's phone lit up with a XinBō panda mailman on a clumsy bike delivering an envelope. Beneath was a message from Ra1nwater saying, "Read THIS. Got posted last night". Ava unlocked her phone and tapped the notification. XinBō opened up and displayed a screenshot of a post on Twip from Marissa Knight, Roma's friend and co-conspirator. At first, Ava wondered why her best friend would send such a screenshot but she read on. There were almost a hundred emotion reactions, hearts and tears with a couple likes piled on. A large, black heart graced the profile picture:

I feel like I can't carry on...my ♥ is cryin rn...Ain't no body gotta feel what I feel rn. Let em know everyday that hyou love em. I don care how stupid that sound...let em know cuz...one day they not gon be her an you gonna wonder iff there's something you said or something.

Heart breakin too much, ain't have to happen. Romi, you ♥ from above now... should nvr been you.

A chill drew over Ava, her mind reeled. *Wait, what- is she ... Is Roma dead?* Ava messaged back:

>**Wix23**: is she ded
>**Wix23**: dead*

In seconds, an answer.

>**Ra1nwater**: Looks it
>**Ra1nwater**: Kilt herself
>**Wix23**: WHAT
>**Ra1nwater**: There's suppo to be a note smwhr

Ava couldn't believe her eyes. *Roma ... just killing herself? How?* Roma never struck Ava as a depressive type. She thought Roma quite enjoyed being evil and malicious, that she existed on it. But now, Roma was dead. Dead by her own hand. No more walking past cackling in the halls. No more worrying about getting jumped in the bathroom. No more getting tripped up the stairs or mocked when she spoke. Years and years of terror and torment, gone overnight. And hopefully shall never be replaced.

Ra1nwater: Here it is

Another screenshot popped up, this time from a Roma Wilbur. Her profile picture looked recently changed. It was now a duck-face girl posing in a blotchy bathroom mirror cast in black and white with a little black ribbon in the corner. Her skin was medium dark and her face was round but sharpened to an oval at the chin. Her plump cheeks were sucked in; her short, permed hair pulled back flat into a spiky ponytail that stood up stiff from the back of her head. Roma in her best pose, she looked into the mirror like a wannabe model. It was no secret that Roma was self-absorbed, vapid and braggadocious. To Roma, those were her best traits. Over a hundred tear reactions with a few likes and hearts peppered in.

> I'm sorry for what I did to this world. I'm sorry for being alive. Everything I do is awful. Why am I even here? Why? I have to leave now. Don't mourn me. I would have never done the same for you.

Lexi sent a confused emoji.

> **Ra1nwater**: I'mma be real
> **Ra1nwater**: This don't sound real
> **Ra1nwater**: Like, this don't sound like her
> **Ra1nwater**: AT ALL

Ava was still held speechless. Two rough hands came up from behind her and gently gripped her arms. Ava jumped and whirled around. It was her father, Jermaine.

His scruffy face twisted with concern, "Everythin' all right? You've been standin' there for a while, baby girl."

Ava checked the door behind him, she couldn't remember if it was open or closed. Jermaine flipped on the light and the bathroom orb's bright bask made Ava squint until her eyes adjusted. Ceramic decals graced the sink and tub, coral tiles lined the floor. Ava brushed off what she read and donned a loving smile.

"I'm fine, Dad. Just was talkin' with Lexi over school stuff," Ava falsely reassured. Ava saw her brother and father the same: overprotective. Better to say nothing.

Jermaine's face softened. "Well, don't stand there like a zombie," he joked, sleep heavy in his gruff voice. "Get ready. Don't be late for school, okay?"

"Ok, Dad," said Ava. Jermaine clapped her shoulders and left. He walked with a haggard gait; his joints hadn't warmed up to the day yet.

Ava turned on the copper faucet and picked out her red toothbrush. She wanted to continue talking to Lexi but an orange away icon sat by Ra1nwater's name. But there were still unread messages.

> **Ra1nwater**: Roma don't talk like this,
> too stuck on herself
> **Ra1nwater**: And look

Attached was another screenshot, again from Marissa. It had fewer reactions, posted perhaps an hour ago:

> Ain't no body gonna tell me she killed herself. Romi not like that at all liiiiiiike do you know her? Her note ain't real. Somebody killed her and posted that nonsense on her phone. Police stay lyin! Electrocution? Wht? Prolly tased her when nobody was lookin'. She ain't kill herself and whoever did is about to get found out. I'm a wolf, I am comin'!

> **Ra1nwater**: Byron got mutual friends
> with her so he's been
> sending me these
> **Ra1nwater**: But they prolly all over
> school now tho
> **Ra1nwater**: Marissa always gotta be
> extra ¬_¬

43

Ra1nwater is Away

Dread no longer held Ava but malaise certainly did. She knew the school would be filled with gossip, fake condolences and grief counselors – all of her least favorite things. A year or two ago, a student died in a car accident and the atmosphere of Melissa Elliot High School for about two weeks was absolutely insufferable. So many people regaled stories and memories of someone most of them never knew, just to fit in. Truth be told, the student was a nobody that no one cared about and then he died, the end. He was more loved dead than when he was alive. The ones who actually knew him remembered him as a boring, introverted social outcast who pined to have friends but had less presence than a shadow at midnight. It was all one long, aggravating act.

And so it would be for Roma. Gone and ignored would be Roma's penchant for hall fights, picking on others, and cursing out both teachers and administrators alike. Erased and forgotten would be her flippant ways and shell of a heart. She would be an angel instead, one who had never done any wrong. Once, Roma mocked a visiting speaker for their lisp as they retold the story of how they got their hearing back through medical advancement but now that would be passionately dismissed in lieu of a nicer, humbler and more wonderful person.

I'd rather skip, Ava thought.

Ava went to school but she didn't stay for long. Already murmurs drifted through the bus among the students as she and her brother rode in. The only reason she even left was because she traveled to school with Tyrone and knew he wouldn't let her stay home. They always rode together in the morning, him ushering her out the house. Though, it did strike her that Tyrone was quieter that morning. She didn't think much of it, though. All Ava wanted was to be off that bus and away from the maddening crowd. And perhaps collect Lexi; she too was oft tormented by Roma.

She scanned the sleepy crowd in front of the school. Students commonly collected around the slabstone pony wall in front of the school – but no Lexi. Not even Byron, who Ava was sure Lexi had a small crush on. Tyrone had already drifted off. Ava never knew where Tyrone went in the morning before classes but she figured probably to the library or in some overlooked stairwell. Spotting no one, Ava gave up looking and sauntered away to a further bus stop to head to Dice & Strips.

In a couple minutes, the 28 South rumbled up and she got on. It would be a short ride to the games and comics store.

Ava loved visiting Dice & Strips on the weekends. She didn't think of herself as much of a nerd but they did sell XinBō Diamond cards, for those who wanted big ticket items or special editions gachas in-app, without the wait of Daily Diamonds. Ava liked collecting them for their art, no three looked the same. Lexi was a super regular, she rarely visited less than once a week and almost never left without a shopping bag or four. Lexi got on well with the owners as a result. Sometimes they would slip Lexi a spare trinket or two, especially after major release events. Ava also.

The bus squealed to a stop in front of Rex Candor, a pint sized coffee shop that hadn't changed since the '80s - well, the flickering "open" sign may have been from the turn of the millennium. Next door was Dice & Strips, their two large windows bright with reflected sunlight on that cloudless day. As she stepped off the bus onto the busy sidewalk, a notification chimed. Ava placed her phone on silent and checked the messages while she strolled in.

> **Ra1nwater**: Whr RU?
> **Ra1nwater**: Ty is *frekin* creapy! And Mariisa gon crazy
> **Ra1nwater sent a video**
> **Ra1nwater**: She gone nuts! And Ty bening weird cuz you not here!

Ava sighed and pocketed her phone. Though Ava did not know the owners as well, one thing she did know was their leniency towards truancy - unless you were noisy, stealing and/or troublesome. Then you were *out*. Usually in the hands of police. But if you stayed out the way in a forgotten corner and blended? You were just fine. And that was the plan: stay out of sight, finish homework, survive the day and go home.

Ava scanned the store, few people were there. Weekday mornings never attracted a crowd. Stacks and racks filled with countless, vibrant books, boxes of board games, and rows of toys. The walls were fun colors but quite blank. The shelves were random, some lined the walls, some curled into a spiral, others stood about. A life-size Vixen statue stood by the short line of registers, wearing a jet blue party hat. On the other end of the sale counter, stood a cardboard cutout of Amadeus Cho wearing Hulk fist toys, posed with a confident smile and a handwritten "Welcome to our Store!" tacked above him. Behind the registers stood a sleepy college kid with dreads and a Black Lightning shirt. He yawned and looked out the window, watching the morning crowd mill about and wishing he wasn't one of them. Soft ambient music played from above.

Ava went straight for one of the spiraling stacks, walking its depths to the very end where all the older games and comic-based novels lived. Few people visited that area, which was fantastic for Ava. She parked herself against the very back of the spiral, slipped out her phone, threw off her bookbag and took a breath. But her blinking phone kept catching her eye.

The dot flashed various colors, messages coming from many different places. She would've bet at least 98% of them came from Lexi.

It's just gonna have to wait. Ava just wanted a break from her life. She had never once heard Lexi say anything about her brother that didn't gravitate towards negative, even when he was nice. Besides, Marissa's nearest and dearest partner-in-crime just died, of course she would be out of sorts. For once, Ava just wanted some breathing room from life itself. One day's distance wouldn't make the world end. However way they were acting today, they would be the same tomorrow. *Same song, different day. It's all just going to be on repeat forever and ever*, Ava seethed as she fished through her backpack for the rest of her Latin homework. After she pulled that out and found a pen at the bottom of her messy bag, Ava put the phone aside in an open bookbag pocket and started finishing her work.

Chapter 3

Sept 24, 2015

Mood: Tired, Angry

I think God hates me or something right now. Like, *nothing* is going *anywhere* and too much is happening right now. Too much. Teeeeeeeeeeeeew much, ok?

Roma died. Like, she offed herself. I mean, I don't know how to feel but I guess glad? She was *evil*. I hate...d? Hated? Wahtever, can't, couldn't and never could stand her. I wanna say she had it coming, maybe she finally thought about all she done and it all got her all at once but hey, that's all her. She was an awful girl that was *forever* messing with others. Like always. Forever and ever. She was prolly born mean. I can't feel sorry for her.

And now Marissa wanna act big like she gonna be a detective and "track down Romi's killer." It's her, chick. She dead. Did it to her self. Even blamed cops like this another BLM moment. Is she serious? So dramatic and now mad she lost the only person she'd wanna talk to and now gotta find someone else to suck up and be fake with. Suicide contagion is a thing, maybe I'll get lucky. They both were horrible and evil.

I know these ain't nice things to say but they ain't nice people. They don't deserve kind words. The only thing that stops them from being a terror is death itself so , hey, I'm taking what I can get out of this. Some peace and quiet!

Ava posted on "Private". The gray eye blinked and Ava exhaled with a great sigh. The release felt as if she had held her breath for hours. Her homework was finished, she was away from the misery that lit up her phone, she even still had a good bit of the afternoon left. For once, she was exalted and content. She tipped her head against the books and wondered when all this would end – when life wouldn't be hard, trying or terrifying. Yes, college was on the horizon but sometimes that sounded like a new, angry beehive of problems and not the finishing line of education that her teachers and administrators promised. Ava couldn't help but to wonder.

Ava checked the time: 1:15 PM. *Almost time to go home*, Ava noted as she gathered her things. There wasn't much, she made a small camp. She only took out what she needed and used her bag as a lumpy pillow. With everything gathered together and pulled onto her lap, Ava decided to see what storm awaited her and checked her phone.

Lexi had a horrific day. Police, medic, ambulance, you name it, they came. Except for priests, who probably should have been called first and only.

Her day began with waiting for Ava on the stone slab pony wall but a charming voice piped up behind her.

"If it isn't Lexi the sexy," crooned Byron. He had a lightning smile, gold tipped short dreads and skin darker than midnight. He was her Chemistry II lab partner and had a penchant for competitive gaming. He loved sharing his latest stats with her during boring lectures.

Lexi grew a wide grin as she turned around. He crushed on her hard and she didn't mind it. He wasn't awful to look at and his mind was appealing. "Hey, Byron."

He gave Lexi a warm hug, "Everything's all over the school now." He pulled out his phone, it had a crack drawn along the side. Byron scrolled through his various feeds for Lexi to see, "Twip, Twitter, it's everywhere! People goin' straight *wild* over this." He noticed a small crowd amassing around them. Eavesdroppers. "Hey, though, I got a new game. The sun's too bright on my phone to show it to you, wanna go inside?"

Lexi picked up quickly, "Yeah, what game is it?" Even at conventions, she was never big on crowds. Especially nosey ones.

Byron answered as they went onward towards the school, "Some new action game a dev let me have early access to." A half tone louder, he continued, "It's called 'Gossip Folks'."

Lexi stifled a snicker as parts of the crowd dissipated.

Inside, Lexi and Byron found an empty, unlocked classroom in the back hall. There, Byron resumed showing Lexi the complete play-by-play on his Twip timeline.

"Roma posted her thing at about 2:53 AM. Ain't nobody really look at it until morning, when everybody started gettin' up. My boy Chico friends with her so I got all the inside looks. Marissa over here goin' off first. She posted that at abooooooooooout ... 5:28, basically 5:30 in the mornin'. The *second* post – now the second post, you ain't gonna find that no more, she deleted it or somethin'. Maybe somebody said somethin', maybe she tryna be 'composed'" – Lexi let out a snort at his playful air quotes – "or whatever. Either way, it ain't up there no more. Buuuuuut, you know how everything stays forever on the internet," he flashed a toothy smile as he ribbed Lexi's side. She beamed back.

The phone bleated out a harsh trumpet tap. It was an

email from the school. Lexi's phone sang out a raucous, short melody in her back pocket. She checked it, it was also from the school. Byron opened his and they skimmed it together. It was from Ms. Ableton, the principal:

> Today is a sad day for all of us at Melissa Elliot H.S. #28. Today we have lost one of our own, Roma Wilbur. She was a Junior that pursued bioethics and fashion. Her vibrant personality lit up a room and she always made her presence known as a future leader.
>
> As it appears, many of our student body has learned of Ms. Wilbur's passing via social media. It is regrettably true that Ms. Wilbur took her own life last night. We, the administration, would like to remind students that if they need someone to talk to, please reach out. You are not alone. To lead the future, we all must be there. Counselors will be available and on standby for anyone who is in need.
>
> We would like to extend our condolences, thoughts and prayers to the parents and loved ones of Ms. Wilbur. She will be dearly missed.

Lexi and Byron gave each other a bemused look and then broke out in laughter. They continued scrolling until classes began.

Throughout the day, Lexi tried and tried again to get ahold of Ava. Ava had never ever ghosted her before. Nor was she the type to skip, she only did it twice before and both times were because her cramps were bad enough to make her nauseous. Lexi figured the Roma news must have really struck her and hoped she was okay. Tyrone, on the other hand, seemed to be any and everywhere.

Lexi hurried down the hall to her next class, Drama. No matter where she went or what she did, Tyrone crossed her path. Passing her in the hall, traveling the stairs, reviewing a nearby bulletin board. Always around somehow. She didn't bother to wonder if he knew where Ava was, or if he knew she was gone. He revolted her, how he always wrapped himself around his sister like a constrictor. *Maybe some distance would do him some good*, she spat to herself. She hadn't seen him so far during her run to the next class.

She pulled out her phone, encased in a large, rubber strawberry case. Still no sign of Ava. No text, no phone, not even XinBō. She checked Wix23's account, it had been idle since the early morning, since their last conversation. *This ain't like Ava at all –*

Tyrone plucked Lexi's phone out of her hands as he breezed by her. Lexi chased after Tyrone as he opened Lexi's text messages to fire a quick "Where are you, baby sister?" to Ava and plopped it back into Lexi's hands without breaking his stride. He continued stalking down the hall as Lexi stared holes into him, angry and befuddled. She wanted nothing more than to shout curses at him ... but she'd rather have him be a passing storm. Lexi looked at the text and sent one behind it, "That came from yur psycho bro. HE TOOK MY PHONE. WTF?! Say somthin'!"

Steamed, Lexi shoved the phone back into her pocket before Tyrone could return and darted off to her second period class.

Drama was quiet and boring, a couple reviews of *Joe Turner, Come and Gone* but a sickening scream outside the red double doors broke the tedium. Then there was a crowd of responding screams. No shots, it wasn't a shooting. Lexi ran to the double door windows and tried to glimpse outside. Standing bodies crowded her view and shadowed the doors. Her teacher, Mr. Thompkin, called her back but she ignored him and pushed out against the throng to squeeze through the crowd. Sifting through the murmuring, curious swarm, Lexi broke out into the front. What she witnessed horrified her.

There stood a bloody, sliced up Marrisa, clutching a jagged shard of bathroom mirror. Her dark brown eyes were dazed and distant. She gripped the shard harder, everyone could see it slice deeper into her copper mahogany hand. She was in absolute tatters. Her left arm bore a deep gash on the inside of her forearm almost extending from elbow to wrist. It hung limp and dripped with a steady stream of blood. There were smaller slashes and cuts along her skinny legs and shoulders.

No one could get close to her. She looked out of it but always gave a clean swipe at whoever tried to approach her, even from behind. Blood flung with every slash, and people ambled to get back. A few were struck with splatters and broke out in hysterics. A couple beads landed on the cuff of Lexi's sock.

Unaware of the spray, Lexi took out her phone to record the chaos. Ava had to see this: Marissa flat out her mind, howling wild.

"I deserve this!" Marissa shrieked. Her gold wrapped braids whipped around her, wet and disheveled, her voice hoarse. "I *hate* me! I ... I ..." She staggered out quietly to herself, "Why, why am I *doin'* this? I ... My ... I can't think straigh–" then Marissa snapped back into roaring in a daze, "I am *nothing*!" She slashed at herself again, everyone screamed. "Nothing! Nothing! Nothing!" Marissa punctuated every cry with another deep slash on her body. She was a terrible mess of blood. No one wanted to touch her, no one wanted to be near her.

There were a couple cries from the crowd: "Put down the knife!" "Please don't hurt yourself anymore!" "Roma wouldn't want this!" None reached Marissa. At least, not at first. Her daze broke again, and she winced deeply with pain. All over her body, she witnessed red pouring out of her like a vase. She was startled at her limp, shredded arm, her sliced shirt and pants. She sucked in deep, teary breaths – then snapped back to her daze. "I *deserve* this!" she screamed at the top of her lungs.

A school safety officer, a portly, tubby man with dyed brown hair popped through the crowd and barked out from behind Marissa, "No you don't! Let's *talk* about this, you and I. I just need you to turn aroun-"

"I'm sorry for being alive!" Marissa cried out with sheer agony. She drew in a wet, ragged gasp and bellowed, "Please don't stop me! I'll always be this way! I'm no different than *Roma*!" Without a glance, Marissa swung her bloody glass shard behind herself at the charging officer. He tried to take her unawares but instead sprang back with his eye covered as Marissa wailed out, "I have to do this to me! I *have* to!" She beat her leg with her fist in grief, stabbing it with the shard in punctuation, "You! Don't! Un! Der! *Stand*!" Marissa broke out of her daze for a moment but snapped back, roaring, "I hurt *so* many! I'm just like Roma!"

They tried to refute her but she screamed over them, "You know *nothing*! Sheep and fools and *idiots*!" The crowd pleaded louder.

Marissa stopped cold upon seeing Lexi's camera. She grew quiet and still. The crowd grew quiet along with her, all noise slipped into silence. Her unsteady eyes, her wild stare, Marissa was at war with herself. Blood pattered to the floor from her rattling fingertips. The glass was bathed so deeply in red-orange it bore no more reflection. The school officer whispered in support on his radio, he tried to tell nearby students he may need help tackl-

"This is for you."

Marissa swept the shard of glass cleanly and deeply across her throat from ear to ear. Her head hung back, and blood fell like a waterfall over her soaked chest as she stabbed herself in the side twice, leaving the shard there with only an inch or three to grab. Everyone erupted into terror at her fallen body.

Lexi fled. She couldn't get what she saw out of her mind. Thundering down the stairwell, she sent the video to Ava. Reaching the bottom, Lexi tucked herself in a corner and called her father, Phil, who worked closest at the post office as a mail sorter. Her mother, Shannon, was much further away, working at a pier fixing fish sensors and doing marine repairs for local boats.

Phil picked up on the second ring, a bit hushed so his ever-present manager couldn't hear him, "Baby, I'm –"

"Daddy," Lexi blurred out in Tagalog, "please come *get* me! I wanna leave, I wanna *leave*! Somebody just killed themselves in front of me!"

Ava sat in a daze of her own, her eyes wide and her mouth agape. She watched the video with her headphones on. Ava could hear Lexi's screams cut clear over the crowd when Marissa did the unthinkable.

With jittery fingers, Ava stopped the video and called Lexi. It didn't even dial a full ring before Ava heard a sobbing, whining voice.

"Omigaaaaad, Avaaa. She did it right in front of me!"

Ava didn't know what to say. She felt awful Lexi had to experience that alone, front and center. "Are - are you ok? Are you safe?"

"Nooooo!" Lexi squealed in anguish. "I'm - home. Dad got me - he - he - I saw someone *die*! I just - oh my god, Ava, where *were* you?"

"I ... I ...." Ava's jaw bobbled, her mind was blank from the shock of it all. "I tried to find you - you this mornin', you weren't - weren't there. I - I ... oh my god ..." Ava smeared a hand down her face, she had no decent excuse. "Lexi, I skipped, I wish I had found you -"

"No!" Lexi pierced. Ava was silent. They both were. Ava tried to speak again but Lexi shot her down again with another sharp, "No!" Lexi then broke into a full sob.

Ava remained silent. Guilt flooded through her. She heard distant Tagalog in the background on Lexi's side. It was Lexi's father, he had a tone of saddened compassion.

Choked up, Lexi feathered out, "I'll - I'll talk to you later." She hung up.

Ava took a breath for herself but she had no time to deal, Tyrone was ringing. Ava picked up and feigned an upbeat demeanor, "Hey, Ty -"

"Baby sister," Tyrone's calm voice carried a suppressed irritation underneath. "Oh, how I missed you, my dearest heartbeat. Where have you been all day? The darkness hints to me where you are and I'm not sure whether I like it or believe it. Where. Are. *You*?"

Oh, here we go, Ava worried. Tyrone always brought up "the darkness" and what it hinted to him when he didn't know where she was. And whenever he mentioned "the darkness", the air always seemed to grow thicker, almost choking her. Ava hated it, she despised her wheezing panic attacks.

"I – I skipped," she admitted. A light wheeze winded between her words. The phone grew hot as she clutched it tighter. The boom was coming and she knew it. The wheeze became a bit stronger, she was sure it was a full-blown panic attack.

"Come home," Tyrone sighed. His mounting anger passed into steam. The air leavened around Ava. "I love you, baby sister. Come home." Tyrone hung up.

Ava coughed as her lungs felt release. This was almost as bad as the time she wandered off in a mall from him. She thought the air would crush her as she heard him call out to her. Tyrone found her crumpled on the floor of a pet shop begging for breath. It only stopped once she was in his arms. Ava remembered what Tyrone told her, "I found you through the darkness, baby sister. You know better than to leave my side. You'd die without me." He kissed her forehead and bought her ice cream afterwards.

Regained of steady breath, Ava shook off the memory, pocketed her phone and got up. She had to bend over to accommodate the sudden head rush she got but she eventually threw on her backpack and with a staggered stumble, left the store.

Chapter 4

Ava came home an hour later. Nothing about the day seemed real, nothing seemed to match. The terror and blood seen on her screen; the quiet of the comic store. The casual stroll of the bus down the street; the pandemonium blipping all throughout her feeds. There were even glimmers on XinBō. The world she saw through her phone and the world around her was a jarring, unsettling match. As if nothing happened, as if it was all some very intricate and terrible movie.

The house was quiet. Her footsteps resounded with light taps as she hesitantly padded through the door. The lights were off, the television dark. Only daylight ebbed through the living room in its late afternoon light.

"Over here, baby sister," invited Tyrone. His voice caught Ava off guard, her back tapped into the wall.

Dread filling her, Ava closed the door and slipped her bag down next to it. She walked to the couch with a prisoner's gait. She found Tyrone, eyes focused on the blank TV, annoyed, tired and waiting. He had on a dark navy shirt and khaki pants, Ava could clearly see his tense shoulders and building disappointment.

Without a word, Ava sat next to her brother. Clenched and still, she tried to still her shallow breath. Tyrone remained silent and unchanged, eyes still on the television.

The silence killed her, she wanted to secure some mercy. Ava laid her head upon his shoulder, draped her arm over his stomach and looked up at him with baleful eyes. The air became a little dense.

"You *skipped*," growled Tyrone. Ava tensed up.

Out she stuttered, "I'm – I – I got – Somethin' happened today." Ava cast her eyes down in shame, her forehead nestled against Tyrone's neck. She felt a light spark, a sharp twinge on her hand as Tyrone scooped it up.

"Don't do that again," he chided. His voice was so cold. Ava felt another spark on her clasped hand as her brother drew out, "Baby sister, I do *so* much for you and yet, this is what I get. Do I not love you enough?"

The air built more pressure, isolating and growing. "You do," she breathed out. She felt the air harder to take in.

"Do I not *care* for you enough?"

"Y-you care. You care deeply," Ava hurried out. A light wheeze carried under her words.

"Do I not *love* you enough?"

Ava paused, dredging for breath. She felt another spark. It astonished her how bad her nerves were. The jolts were always as bad as her suffocating panic attacks, she despised them as well. Tyrone always knew how to have her completely unraveled, she knew that. Ava threw out, "I love you with all my heart."

"Why?" Tyrone drew out even longer. He had a growing wry smile.

Worried her nerves would give her another spark, Ava hurried, "You are my protector and my friend. I'd die without you." Ava rasped for air. This answer always spared her, always curried favor. She hoped it would in this moment, the world felt like it was closing in and growing dark.

Tyrone chuckled and turned to his sister and scooped up her chin. "Then ... why did you skip?" He stared down at his ailing sister. To her struggle for breath, her begging gaze, her onset of tears, he returned only unfeeling, disdainful scorn. "I only want the truth, baby sister." His flatness became a mocking plea, "Please? You'll make your big brother cry if you don't." He pouted at her struggling face before breaking into a slow smile.

Ava could barely speak, the air was so thick. She had to force out her words. "Roma ... died. Marissa ... a video of her ...."

"How'd they die?" Morbid interest rolled from his tongue. He shifted himself to face Ava, his finger still hooked under her chin. "What did you see in the video? Was it *clear*?"

"Roma ... killed herself ... Marissa ... the same? She ... she cut herself–" Ava wanted to cough but dared not to.

"Where?" Tyrone's face grew closer. He enjoyed every passing moment of this.

Ava choked out, "Her ... her arm ... and neck. Ty ... I can't breathe. Can I ... lay down?"

Tyrone spilt out more mock concern, "Oh, my baby sister. Are you not feeling well? Do you not *love* me enough? Is that it?"

Chest burning, Ava pled, "Ty, help me!" The air felt so crushing, the world started to fade into darkness. "I'll never do it again!"

The darkness lifted. Ava dragged in new breath as Tyrone broke away into a small fit of laughter. Ava was confused but concerned herself more with being able to breathe again all the same.

Wiping a tear, Tyrone sighed to himself, "The things I do for you." As Ava sat there in clueless wonderment, Tyrone offered, "You want anything to eat?"

Ava didn't answer, she was still gathering her breath. Tyrone didn't care, he pecked her on the forehead and launched up off the couch to stroll into the sun-lit kitchen. The day still looked lovely outside through the storm door. He rifled through the fridge and cabinets, searching for anything quick or ready to eat. In the top cabinet, he happened upon some cereal snack bars and crowded a pile into his hands. Leaving the kitchen, the open cabinet door breezed shut behind him.

"Have a cereal bar." He skimmed the wrappers and spotted a few particular ones. He offered the pile to his sister, "Here, I found your favorite. It's the red wrappers." Tyrone sounded kind and loving, a stark contrast to who he was a moment ago.

Ava saw the red wrappers in the pile and carefully pulled them out to hold in her lap. She looked up at Tyrone's cheery, compassionate face and asked, "What is going on, big brother?"

He loved being called "big brother". With a wide smile, he replied, "I'm caring for you, baby sister."

Ava couldn't help but be taken further aback. She still had a light heave to her chest as she tried to make sense of it all, "It's just ... nothin' makes any sense. This ... this whole day don't make any sense. Why did Roma and Marissa–"

"They picked on you, it's over," he summed up simply. Tyrone plopped down on the couch beside her, the rest of the cereal bars piled in his lap. He picked up a red wrapper from Ava's pile and unwrapped it for her. "They're both done. New day, new way. Now, bite."

He presented a multi-colored marshmallow bar with bits of sugar oats before her. Ava took a slow, small bite from the corner. Tyrone bit off the next piece with more vigor.

Between chews, Tyrone explained, "Y'know ... I can't

be watching out for you forever. I'm bushed!" He offered Ava another bite, which she took.

"Did ... did you – did you have something to do with it... big brother?" Ava asked.

Tyrone relished the moment, he couldn't keep the joy off his face. "Ava, baby sister." He draped an arm around her slumped shoulders as he continued, "We're both different from the world. I didn't do much, I just helped them realize the errors of their ways. They took it seriously, problem solved." Tyrone took another bite. Left with the final bite in his hands, Tyrone picked it from the wrapper and offered it to Ava, "Say 'ahhhh ....'"

Ava opened her mouth, her mind awash with questions, and received the final piece. Before she could inquest further, Tyrone bubbled at her, "Your cuteness is toxic! This is the baby sister I love and adore. Don't fret your beautiful mind over today. Just know that I'm here and always for you."

Dinner was in front of the TV, again. Ava and Tyrone sat in the middle of the couch together, dishes of pulled pork and asparagus in their laps. A comedy show picked by the twins played, the pair occasionally laughing along. Jermaine was deep in his easy chair, sometimes chuckling along with them. In the kitchen, Yvonne had fixed her plate and looked for a soda to pair it with. Both parents were unaware of the transgressions of the day, as they rarely checked their non-work emails. The news did pick up on the matter but they never cared for news broadcasts, either. They had enough going on in their lives, no need to keep up on which dirty politician said what, who was at war with who. No need to induce more depression, Jermaine and Yvonne could look at their table of bills if they wanted to experience that. At least they could do something about the bills on the table – even if barely. There was nothing they could do about the world.

Ava nestled her head on Tyrone's shoulder as the commercials played. Tyrone rested his head against her crown, his cheek cushioned by her long braids. Yvonne walked into the living room with her plate in one hand and a cold soda in the other.

Seeing her children in harmony, she cooed with a slight Southern twang, "Awwwwww, ain't that sweet? Y'all must really be twins, y'all never bicker or anything."

Tyrone beamed proudly at his mother as she sat on the end of the couch. Ava just watched her mother, unchanged.

As Yvonne settled her food on her lap, Tyrone said, "I can't help it. I love my sister." He gazed down at Ava with adoring eyes, "We're on the same wavelength."

"You think you can let her go when it's time to get married? Can't be wrapped around her forever, Ty," Jermaine joked.

"Dad, I'm sure I will when the time is right," Tyrone assured him with a warm smile.

Ava chimed in, "Daddy, Ty's just lookin' out for me. He's not gonna scare away anyone from dating." Ava laughed, Ty didn't. He kept a plastic smile at Jermaine.

Yvonne shoveled in a fork full of asparagus. "Honey, my brother watched after me a lot. Y'all even nearly came to blows about it."

"Vonnie, he was bein' normal tough-guy-big-bro protective. Ty goes way overboard sometimes."

"How, Dad?" Tyrone inquired with feigned innocence. Ava glanced up at her brother. He was bristling deep down inside, she knew it.

"Weeeeell," Jermaine lingered as he wracked his brain for suitable examples. "You're very hands-on with Ava." Before Yvonne could successfully interject, Jermaine rushed out, "Inaway! Inaway! In. A. *Way*. In a way, Ty can be handsy with Ava. Boys looking at Ava would think *y'all* two were dating. Same with girls looking at Ty."

As Yvonne tried to get a word in edgewise, Tyrone rebutted with slight agitation, "Well, Dad, we're not. Would you rather me be beating her?"

"Whoa!" Yvonne exclaimed over everyone. "Enough! Ty, your father didn't mean it that way. Mainey, Ty gets a bit too comfy with Ava – hey. Ty. No. Let me finish. – Comfy with Ava *for their age*, but he's always been like this towards her."

Jermaine was taken aback. "Grabbing her waist to get her attention? Gazing into her eyes when he *thinks* we're not around –" Ty tried to intrude but Jermaine spoke over him flatly, "Ty. I *saw* you both at Aunt Bessy's house when you thought no one was in the gameroom. I was comin' down the stairs and I *saw* it. You understand you're *brother* and *sister*, right? It's too much."

The air hung heavy in the silence. The TV flickered and Ava felt pressure gather in the room. Ty was *furious*. Yvonne desperately tried to grab back the reins in the conversation.

"Mainey, *stop*. Ty, *stop*. This subject is *over–*"

Tyrone stood bolt upright and roared at his father, "Old man, you don't understand *anything* about us! I will treat Ava however *I* see fit!"

Still couched back, Jermaine spat, "*Boy*, you ain't her father, *I am*. Let me tell you somethi–"

It was a one-hit kill. Tyrone had gathered electric energy into a ball in the palm of his hand and pointed it at his father. The air smelled of fried flesh and ozone. Ava and Yvonne screamed. Ava scooted away in horror. Yvonne grabbed the back of her shirt collar and both jumped from the couch to flee to the front door.

No matter how hard Yvonne tried, the door would not budge. It was jammed shut, like someone was sucking it closed on the other side.

"Ma! Hurry *up!*" Ava shrieked as Tyrone started slowly towards them. The easy chair smoldered behind him, Jermaine slumped over.

Heartless concern etched Tyrone's face. "Baby sister, why are you *scared*?" He grabbed Ava's arm and wrenched her away from Yvonne.

Yvonne reared against the door and panicked alone. She slid to the floor, screaming for safety and begging for mercy. Tyrone laughed and clutched his frightened sister to his side. Energy bristled from his hand as it rested on her hip. With a firm shake, he said, "You can do this, *too*. Baby sister, look at us. Look at this."

Tyrone raised a hand to Ava's eyes. She rattled with fear. Around it, a darkening mass started to collect. Ava screamed. Yvonne stared at the growing ball, wild eyed and mute. Tyrone kissed Ava's forehead. "This is you, too. We're *so* much different from the world. Different from *her*." Tyrone pointed his shadowed hand at their mother. Yvonne yelped but nothing happened. Tyrone cracked out a cruel laughter.

"Look at her squirm and beg, baby sister. She's nothing like us. She's just like Dad: *weak*."

Ava's legs gave out, and she crumbled to the floor beside Tyrone's legs. He grasped her arm, shaking her to get up as he chortled out a wild laughter. The air was thick, Ava developed a light wheeze.

Yvonne screamed, "Ty! Please don't hurt her! You love her! Spare her! Spare me–"

"Never." Tyrone struck her dead with an electric shock.

Ava screamed. She cried for her fallen mother, "Mamaaaaa, nooo. Mama, please get up. *Please*!" She tried to wrench her arm away but the grief and air were too great. All she could do was sit there and wail out.

Tyrone gazed down at his fretful sister in blank apathy. He stooped down and softly tried to shush her as he collected her teary face in his warm hands. She didn't want to look at him, but he forced her to face him, his stare deranged and glad.

"Little Ava," he sang with a gentle chime. Ava wanted to look back at the body of her slain mother but Tyrone kept wrenching her back to face him as he kept chiming for her attention, "Ava. Little Ava. Pretty little Ava. Little Ava. Look. At. *Me*." Locked into her eyes, he spoke with a calm and wonderous, ominous delight, "Oh, my precious heartbeat. Cry no more, for I am here." He kissed her forehead and both her cheeks. Ava tried to stifle her tears.

Tyrone continued, "Come upstairs." Ava shook her head but Tyrone insisted, "You must." He rose but Ava remained on the ground, shambled by terror.

Ava sobbed and wept before him. She could still feel the phantom shadow of his fingers on her face. Her mother's body slumped in the corner of her eye.

A strong draft of wind encircled Ava, pushing her upward and onto her feet. Tyrone took her up from the draft and cradled her in his arms like a bride. As he held her close, Tyrone could feel her quake and shiver. He chuckled softly as he turned towards the stairs and climbed them, "You can move things with your mind, create ice, and make fire but you're shaking. You're being too cute right now."

Ava watched the stairs drift past her. Her mind lingered on his hands curled around her. She understood nothing. *What is he talking about? Make fire?*

Tyrone nuzzled her with kisses to her crown as he

carried her to his room, his door swung open with the sudden breeze. Dark, sparse and lifeless, that was Tyrone's room. No decorations, just some school work strewn about. His tablet laid on his neat, maroon bed. A pile of clothes laid crumpled in a far corner.

He laid Ava on his bed, the tablet slid into her hip.

I have to leave, I have to leave, chambered in Ava's head. Her body still buzzed numb and weak, her throat raw. *I have to leave*.

Tyrone picked up his tablet and went to his pile of clothes to dig something out. He pulled out a dark and pointed item, it bore a chrome glint. He went back to the bed to crawl in beside Ava, pinning her to the wall, "Baby sister, my dear heartbeat. Please know that I love you more than life itself. I would never hurt you, it would be like hurting myself. I adore you too much for that. I am your protector and your friend. I am your shield. I am part of you."

Nestled close, he draped an arm across her and kissed her cheek. He continued, "We have always been like this, our powers. It started when I was four and I stepped through a shadow to get into another room. Do you remember when I told you that?" Ava nodded, she watched him steadily from the corner of her eye. "And how you didn't believe me because I couldn't recreate it in front of you?" Ava kept still. "I thought it was only me for years until one day, your finger bled. We were ten, you were crying. You didn't want to get blood on your very pretty dress and I hated to see you cry. Do you remember what I did?" Tyrone paused and propped himself up over Ava, calmly waiting for an answer.

Ava didn't want to meet his gaze but he hooked her chin gently and steered her eyes over to his.

"What did I do?" Tyrone asked again.

Voice rasped and pained, Ava answered weakly, "You put your mouth on it–"

"I *sucked* it, yes," Tyrone confirmed, very pleased. "I sucked the excess blood off your finger because we couldn't find a bandage. And, my god, what a rush that hit me! I could move things with my mind, I could make fire, make ice – I could travel from place to place without *shadows*. I. Was. *God*. – I was *you*. *You* with *me*.

"But only for a short time. I think a week or so. Then I was back to my same old self. But I was left with a hunger. A hunger for more. A hunger for blood. *Your* blood." Ava's eyes widened.

Tyrone sighed, "I tried to tell you but you wouldn't believe me! Even when I pointed it out, you still didn't believe me. But you became my tender love that day. My crippling addiction. Your blood, my blood, we could become stronger together and rule whatever we want, baby sister." Tyrone placed a hand over his twin's belt buckle. It was warm, heavy and still, "I keep track of your cycle."

Ava's stomach churned with disgust, she looked away to hide this.

He returned her to his eyes. He didn't care about her sneer as he continued, "To know when best to bleed you without making you woozy. Periods don't give up enough blood to sustain me so fear not, your spent pads and tampons are safe. But ..."

Tyrone pulled his hand from her and reached into the narrow gap between them. He pulled out an ornamental knife and held up to the light for Ava to witness its brilliance. It bore soft rippled carvings in the hilt, the sharp of the blade was almost blue. A cold chill gathered over Ava's soul at the realization of what was soon to happen. She scooted closer to the wall with what little strength she could muster, but she was already well pressed against it.

"You. Me. Today is a wonderful day to become one and grow powerful togethe–"

Darkness. Ava had no idea where she was but she saw a thin strip of light cast across her feet. It was crowded, tight and soft. She moved her foot and lightly tapped a heeled boot.

Oh my god, I'm in my closet! How'd the hell I do this? Ava sucked in a breath. She metered it out to stay quiet. Her legs wanted to give out again but she willed herself to stand, to wait for any prime opportunity to escape.

She heard Tyrone stalking about at a distance, cursing her name. The air grew a little thick. Suddenly, she felt rushed and a moment later, a blade was on her throat, narrowly missing her jugular. The closet door was still closed, the air was hard to breathe.

"Can't get away from me that easily, baby sister," Tyrone whispered defiantly. "I can feel your presence anywhere. Like always."

The blade tightened against her throat.

"Feel that?" Tyrone asked. "That's gonna make us stronger. You can't see it but it's up against my throat, too. I'm only gonna make a small cut; deep enough to bleed. You and I can drink each other's blood together, like brother and sister."

Against the biting pressure of the blade, Ava said through clenched teeth, "Never."

"Aww," Tyrone replied with mock sadness. "You just broke my heart. You're still mine, though." He gave Ava a light kiss on the lips and snatched the knife between them.

Ava felt her neck searing and wet. The shock sent Ava to the bathroom, she tumbled down on the rim of the bathtub, clattering the pineapple shower curtains and springing a couple rings. She had struck the back of her head on the ceramic. It rang her head with an awful daze. Ava heard her closet door bang open and slam shut. Hurried footsteps raced towards the bathroom. The bathroom door was wide open, she could tell from the light. She scrambled to snatch down the navy towel hanging beside the tub. Ava bundled it against her throat as Tyrone stormed in. He, too, had a slash upon his neck, the weeping blood poured down onto his darkening collar.

He announced as he came upon her, "I'm gonna get you, you little, ungrateful bit–"

Ava clutched his shirt and dragged him down into the tub with her. She sucked on his flooding wound for a few seconds. This revolted her just as much as the kiss but she had little other choice. Ava shoved Tyrone away, gasping for air. Her mouth was stained red and tasted of iron. A foreign exhilaration surged within her: Power. New power. Tyrone's power.

Pulling himself out of the tub, Tyrone staggered back with a crazed smile. He panted, "See? Doesn't it feel great? Now, do me."

Ava shrank away inside the tub and quivered her head no. Tyrone's smile fell.

"You used me," he realized to himself.

Ava jabbered out meekly, "I'm sorry, I'm sorry, I'm sorr–"

"YOU USED ME!" Tyrone bellowed. He pulled together a ball of electricity, it was smaller and dimmer now.

Ava did the same with her free hand, but with fire. The brilliance of the flame surprised her. Each shot at the same time.

The air became cool and her back felt softness. Ava crept open her eyes and looked around. The room was small, crowded with art toys and action figures, and everything was nauseatingly cute. Starry, pastel cupcakes covered the sheets. Posters and printed pictures plastered the pop pink door. A little bear fell on Ava from the black bookcase overlooking the bed. It had on a teeny shirt with the Filipino flag and a pan-African flag jutted into its paw. This was Lexi's room.

Chapter 5

Ava still could not understand all that she had done but there was one thing she knew for sure: She was grateful that she landed in her best friend's room, the safest place she knew.

But a terrible thought struck her – *Won't Tyrone come?*

Disturbed by the thought, Ava slid off the twin bed and staggered her way to the door to listen for anything. She held her towel close, her blood almost soaked to the other side. Heavy on her palm, Ava shifted it to prevent smears on the door. Sounds of a normal family wafted from downstairs. No death. No mayhem. Just the clinking of plates, warm laughter and a jubilant mixture of English and Tagalog.

"Ma!" Lexi called out. "Dad wants you to help him with the tv! We're gonna watch something!" She sounded brighter than she did on the phone. Ava's heart sank a little.

"Like what, babe?" Her mother called back. Her voice was warm with a Bronx accent.

"Tatay, what are we watching?" asked Lexi.

A thick Manila-accented voice replied with light frustration, "Probably a cartoon movie! ... If I can get this remote to work – Wait. Wait. There it goes. Movie night is a go! Now, we are *getting* somewhere!"

Ava's breath pattered. This family was innocent, and she basically brought death to their door. But where else should she go? Where else *could* she go? And who isn't to say that Tyrone would not have stopped here *anyway* in a relentless hunt for his lost, beloved baby sister?

The least I could do is try to protect them, Ava decided. She reached for her phone in her back pocket to see the time – but it wasn't there. It was back home in her bookbag under her mother's slumped body. She clenched her towel as the memory of the murder flashed in her mind. Her mother's fearful screams rang in her ears. The smell of the shocked flesh. *Little Ava. Pretty little Ava –*

Ava sucked in a quick breath and looked about. She spotted a cloud-shaped wooden clock sitting on the chaotic, messy tall dresser: 10:25. Ava returned her ear to the door. A movie was well underway, something light and fanciful. The family chattered among themselves. Plenty of time to practice.

Adjusting the towel, Ava went back onto Lexi's bed. The foam sank under her weight as she sat on the edge in effort to collect herself. Scattered mangas were everywhere and littered tissues crumpled around the starry wastebasket, it was clear Lexi was trying to cope the best she could. Ava stared with a tired daze at the lamp next to the clock. It was a snow goddess with midnight skin and ice blue eyes holding a grand, illuminated snow ball. On the other side of the lamp stood a small, pewter picture frame. Stamped at the bottom read "Phillip, Alexandria, Shannon". Stamped at the top bore the family name "Dimaanós". The picture was taken two years ago at a park. Lexi had her father's eyes, her mother's smile and the mix of their complexions, which leaned closer towards her mother's dark brunette skin. Shannon had buoyant, fluffy hair gathered atop her head. Her smile was radiant, her blushed cheeks soft and dimpled. The pouf made her seem taller than her husband but they were roughly the same height. Lexi had yet to hit her growth spurt by this picture. Phillip had short, cropped hair and a rounded face. The years never caught up to him, he had the same youthful look he still dons today.

They look so happy, moped Ava. She sighed and tied her towel around her neck the best she could. It wasn't as secure as it was when she held it with her hands but it held and her hands were free. It was time to begin.

In the beginning, Ava had spotty success. Sometimes she'd get something. Other times, she'd get nothing, looking at her empty hands until she felt ridiculous. But, the more she tried, the better she got. She could conjure a flickering ball of fire, a flexing orb of shadow, a swirling sphere of air, one by one. She managed to float the cloud clock to her hand and back. She arched thin bolts from finger to finger until they formed round in her palm. Ice flickered from her knuckles as they scaled her hands. Through her borrowed abilities, she could sense her brother. He was hurt. And deathly furious. Ava practiced harder.

With steady effort, Ava could hold each element a little longer and a bit stronger with each try. Unless something jarred her, like a city truck or a blasting car radio. Every noise made her jump, her blood started to feel like quicksilver from how many times they disturbed her. She only took breaks when her hands shook too much to concentrate.

How could Ty do this? Ava wondered over and over as she regained stillness. Without thinking, she made the air thick. It wasn't crushing, it was padding but when the familiarity struck her, the air dissipated back to normal. *Wait, he was doing this? To me?* Ava shook her head, *Why'd I never believe him?* All those times he said something, all those times she thought the world closing in were panic attacks, everything. She felt stupid and angry. All at herself. *I could have stopped this, I could have stop ...* Ava raked in a breath. The smell of charred chair filled her nose. She couldn't stop hearing Yvonne's screams.

Quick footsteps cut through the memories. It was Lexi, bounding up the stairs.

Ava froze.

Pulling herself out of shock, Ava peered over the foot of the bed. There was a small cube of space between the foot of the bed and the wall, filled with clutter. There were even things on the window sill, as if the clutter continued itself almost out the window. *Do I hide?* Ava wondered as she scanned the room. Small as a postage stamp. *Can I hide?*

Lexi opened her door. Ava curled up and shut her eyes, and the door tapped against her arm. She didn't know that she had teleported behind the door until she snuck an eye open. She flattened herself against the wall, hoping Lexi wouldn't notice.

Night!" Lexi called from the doorway. The film painted a faint smile on her face but still she was drained. Lexi wasn't sure that sleep would do her any good – or if she could even go to sleep. The day rang in her head over and over again.

She closed the door, there was nothing odd or out of place. Though, her bed gave a raucous thump. Lexi whisked around and found Ava leaping off it, begging her quietly for silence.

"Ava, wha–"

Ava clapped a hand over Lexi's mouth. "Shuuuush! *Please!*" She strained. Lexi nodded, frozen still with wide eyes. "I'm *hiding* from Ty." She slipped her hand from Lexi's mouth, which grew agape.

Lexi whispered, "What did he *do* to you?"

Ava couldn't respond. She choked up.

Tears starting to well, Lexi breathed out, "Oh my god, no." She clasped her arms around Ava, who silently sobbed on her shoulder. As Lexi stroked her head with sorrow, a sickness turned her stomach. The day Lexi feared most finally came. She knew one day Tyrone would snap and act on his urges. Violently. And that she would only be available in the aftermath.

Lexi pecked Ava on the cheek. "That bastard," she streamed with an acidic hiss. "Thaaaaaat dirty bastard," she seethed. A warm moisture seeped onto her shoulder. Lexi broke the embrace to discover blood.

Ava snapped, "Don't *tell* nobody!"

"What?" Lexi whispered, astonished. "Ava, *look at you.* You look *awful.* You're *bleeding.* He needs to go *down.* A doctor gotta take a kit and get a samp-"

"No doctors. No. Doctors," Ava cautioned.

Lexi couldn't believe this, she had enough. "Ava. Tyrone *raped* you-"

"He didn't rape me!" Ava struggled to keep quiet.

"He *didn't*?" Lexi shot back, she could barely watch her tone herself. "Then why are yo-"

Ava summoned a fire ball. Lexi stumbled back in shock. Ava grabbed her best friend's wrist with the other hand before she could clatter into the door.

"Not. A. *Soul*. Must. Know," Ava urged.

Bewildered and afraid, Lexi couldn't take her eyes off the swirling fiery orb swallowing Ava's hand. She reached out to touch it, not believing the warmth already emanating from it. Ava stepped back and shook her head slowly. The fire burned bright but all Ava could feel was gentle energy around her hand.

A parade song danced out from the foot of the bed, rapturing both girls' attention. The fireball flared out from existence. It was Lexi's phone, halfway buried under a smiling ice cream pillow. "Evil Twin" beamed across the front.

Ava's breath shallowed. Panic crackled in her chest. Wretched sobs overtook her as she crumpled down. Ava felt powerless again.

Taking control, Lexi stepped past Ava and hissed, "Lemme do this! Just keep quiet!"

Ava tumbled out under terrible, watery breaths, "He's comin' to kill us, I know it." A light whine escaped her lips. "You don't under*stand*."

Lexi sharply hushed Ava into silence and picked up the phone.

"Hello?" Lexi answered. Her voice was bright. She smeared away her tears and held back her sniffles.

"Lexi," Tyrone chimed back. He sounded sweet but irritation laced his undertone. "Ava is missing. I think she ran away. Is she with you? Mom and Dad had an argument with her and she stormed off."

Her blood boiled but she kept calm. "Ava's gone? When?"

"About an hour ago. She didn't come to you?" Tyrone didn't believe her.

Lexi looked at Ava balled up on her floor, curled up with silent tears. Rage filled her mind but she put on her best act. "Nah. But she ran away? That's so unlike her–"

"I know, right?" Tyrone perked. His voice was aglow with restrained vexation. He cleared it out of his tone. "Please help me bring her home, Lexi. I'd *never* forgive myself if something awful happened to her. We're worried. Ma is just goin' mad waitin' for her to come home and Dad's just the same. I hope she'll come to you."

"I'll let you know if I hear anything." Never had Lexi hated someone so much. Rage heated her chest and flared her throat.

"Please? Tell Ava we miss her so much and that no one is angry at anyone. Things just got a little out of control. Give her a call and tell me if she responds." It sounded like a request but Lexi knew it was an order.

Plugging down her hatred, Lexi complied. "Sure. I'll shoot you a text when I hear back. Talk to you later."

Tyrone hung up.

Lexi stared at her phone. "*Dick*," she spat.

Ava whined out a gentle cry. Lexi threw the phone aside and stooped at her best friend's side.

"Don't tell him I'm here ...," Ava creaked. "Plea-ea-ease. God, don't say nothin'. I don't wanna die."

Lexi curled Ava into her arms and rocked her, "I won't say nothin'. You have my word. He won't know." She brimmed with countless questions but kept them to herself. It's just ... she always thought powers were only in comic books. She patted Ava, "I'mma get you set up here for tonight, okay? And we gotta take care of that neck, too."

Ava nodded. "My neck's fine," she spoke softly. "I just gotta sleep."

"Alright," Lexi agreed. She got up and with haste, cleared the small cube of space at the foot of her bed. Ava sat beside the bed, curled up and quiet as Lexi passed her to visit the closet. She pulled out a black, dragon shaped sleeping bag and laid it down. Half of it jutted out beyond the bed but it fit. Lexi pulled the plush, spike-lined tail and opened the bag. There was a forgotten fuzzy blanket inside.

Ava got up and stepped inside the sleeping bag. It was warm and comfortable. Not much room to move around but she didn't care. Ava laid down and Lexi zipped her up and pulled up the dragon hood over her head.

"Try to sleep, okay?" Lexi smiled weakly. The corners of her lips danced, the sorrow of the sight of Ava was hard to bear. She sniffed and assured, "He don't know you here."

Ava nodded and closed her eyes. Her body was in so much pain. Everything blared. But she tried to sleep.

Lexi picked up her phone and shot off a quick "No signs yet" text to Tyrone as she tapped the foot of her lamp to turn the light off. Already she was in her bed clothes, an oversized Electro Phi Beta shirt and shorts with kitten paws all over.

Lexi piled into bed. Watching the street lights streak

across her ceiling, she didn't know if she could sleep. She sat up to give Ava one last check: the moonlight crossed her tear-streaked face as she laid still as a corpse. Her eyes were winched shut, her mouth turned into a twisted frown. All Tyrone's handiwork.

"*Douchebag*," Lexi spat to herself. She laid back down and tried to get some sleep.

Ava had a dreamless sleep. Her body laid tense and stiff. Frost collected over her wound, sealing it shut with a thin sheet of ice. She was tucked in and folded up. Right before dawn, a gentle shake woke her. Ava's eyes flashed open, and a small jolt of electricity ran through her hair. Lexi kept her hand on Ava's arm and smiled warmly. She was crouched beside her, her natural hair mussed. Ava softened up at the sight and released a deep breath.

"Morning, baby sister," Lexi said alluringly.

Sheer terror rang Ava's heart. She couldn't move, the sleeping bag trapped her. This had to be a nightmare.

"Lexi, nooo," Ava mustered out as she tried to shift away in the small cube of space. There was nowhere she could go.

Lexi gave a sweet chuckle, "I'm just *borrowing* her, baby sister." She reached over and whispered in Ava's ear, "I can still control people." Pulling away, she continued, "Come home, baby sister. You scared me so much when you ran away."

Her wound throbbed with coursing blood. The air grew a slight thickness. Lexi draped herself against Ava and rested her head against Ava's cheek. With a wry smile, she said, "Come home to me, baby sister. No one else has to die. You'll develop bloodlust," mock concern soaked her words. "Then you won't be able to do anything but. I just wanna make it easy for you. Come home."

Rattling, Ava tried to shuffle away. "N-no ... no!" she whimpered. "I *won't*."

Lexi hooked Ava's chin and steered her grey eyes to her own dark browns. Lexi inspected Ava's face, staring down her nose like a cold, disdainful mother. "My god, you look so terrified." Lexi broke into a vicious smile. "Come home to big brother. I'll keep you safe."

"N-no," Ava stammered. A wheeze fell into her words, the air was thicker now.

Lexi's smile fell into a snarl. "I guess you think you got choices, huh?" She looked around. On the windowsill sat a clear paperweight with a daisy suspended inside. She picked it up, testing its heft in her hand. Then she cocked it away from herself, aiming for her forehead.

Before Lexi could bash her skull in, Ava wrung out a hand to clasp around the paperweight. "You will *not* hurt Lexi. Or *anyone*."

Tyrone laughed through Lexi, dismissive and cruel. Through Lexi's eyes he watched his sister peel the paperweight out of Lexi's hand and seal it to the floor with a thick cover of ice. That tickled him more.

"My *god*, baby sister," Lexi tittered, "I was just being funny. I wasn't *really* going to do it." Then Lexi threw herself atop Ava, pinning her with the sleeping bag. Lexi's eyes were cold and unsettling. "Or was I? Baby sister, you know me so well. Tell me."

Hatred started to boil over Ava's fears. Through clenched teeth, she demanded, "Get *off* me, Tyrone. Get out of Lexi and get *off* me." *You murderer*, Ava continued in her mind.

Lexi gave an exaggerated pout, "But you might run away again."

"Tonight," Ava bartered. "Give me until tonight."

Lexi furrowed her brows with a tilted smirk. "But why not now? Baby sister, don't you *love* me?"

"Give me until tonight, big brother," she restated, her voice unwavering. Lexi scowled but Ava continued, "No nothing until tonight. Then ... I'm yours." The thick air dissipated. Her wheeze was gone.

Lexi broke into a wild smile and shifted with delight. "Together?"

"Forever," Ava smirked. "I love you, big brother. You are my protector and friend. I'd die without you."

Lexi pulled herself off Ava, satisfied. Then her face fell blank. She felt confused and light-headed.

Ava sat up and slipped out the sleeping bag, keeping a cautious eye on Lexi. The sleeping bag crinkled in the quiet as Ava sat atop it, ready for anything.

"Lexi?" Ava checked. She wasn't sure she could harm her best friend ... but Tyrone was unpredictable. Traces of electricity ran through her braids in anticipation.

Minding her head, Lexi grumbled, "How'd I get on the floor?"

Tied between telling the truth and telling a lie, Ava chose to fib. "You were sleepwalkin' a little."

Lexi shook and rubbed her head, "Really? Man, seein' Marissa killin' herself really got to me. How'd you sleep?"

Ava shrugged, "Not well."

Sleep still wrapped around her, Lexi squinted her eyes from the morning light, "Hey, did I imagine you having fire around your hand last night?"

"This?" Ava produced a brilliant and roaring fireball, light filled the space. Though she had poor rest, her abilities felt a little more restored and easier to summon.

Lexi reared back. Ava waved the fireball extinguished. Her mother reacted the same way. The air smelled of flesh and –

"No! Bring it back," said Lexi. She padded forward on her palms, an intrigued smile etched on her face.

Has Ty possessed her again? Ava feared. In case he did, she created a strong electric ball, one that would be sure to either impress or intimidate. It crackled softly, illuminating Lexi's wondrous look.

"That's a different one," Lexi breathed. "How many can you do?"

Confirming it was Lexi, Ava stopped the electric current. "I'm still figuring that part out myself."

Lexi looked at Ava's neck. Her towel was gone, shifted off during sleep. The slit on her throat glittered from the dawning light. Blood carpeted the front of Ava's shirt like a red pelt. The handiwork of Ava's cruel brother.

"Why didn't you use it on him?" Lexi pointed.

Ava defended, hurt, "I did. That's how I got away. I can teleport–" Ava appeared sitting on Lexi's bed. "I can control air, shadows, fire, ice and electricity. Ty can do some of this, too."

Lexi's face dropped. The very idea chilled her to the core. "He *what*?"

Ava climbed down from the bed and tried to console Lexi, "I'm gonna handle this. He won't bother either of us ever again."

Lexi still could not process Tyrone having abilities that could easily expand his reign of terror. "You ... what?... What? Are you gonna drop him in the Arctic or something?"

Ava didn't respond. She didn't know what to say. She barely had any semblance of a plan. Instead, she just bowed her head.

"Ava, *how*?" Lexi repeated.

Ava looked up. "I – I don't know. But he'll – he'll kill me if I don't try – he'll kill us. Just ... Just ... me first," Ava trailed off. This was all too much for her. "I have until tonight." Ava looked away. The sun was brighter now, the day was cool.

Lexi tried to follow, "What's tonight? Did Tyrone tell you somethin'? Ava, can't you tell your paren–"

"They're *dead*," Ava snapped. Lexi paused with a sharp gasp. "Ty *killed* them. And *I'm* next." She looked at her hand, spots of darkness swirled around it. "Unless I do somethin'. I have to–"

Lexi threw her arms around Ava. She sniffed and silently cried. Lexi couldn't imagine a day without her family. And judging from Ava's wounds, her parents most likely suffered a merciless death.

Ava pulled Lexi's arms from around her. "Lex, I can't go out there like this. I need practice or I'm dead in the water. Help me?" Lexi couldn't stop crying; Ava gave her a firm shake, "*Help me*?"

Lexi nodded and wrapped herself around Ava again. Ava's eyes grew hot but she couldn't wallow for long.

"I got – I got an idea," Ava said.

Ava needed a clear house. Lexi went into her parents' room and asked to stay home. They unanimously agreed. When it was time for them to head off to work, Lexi met them at the door to kiss them goodbye – and to ensure neither would visit her room. After that easy feat, only Lexi and Ava remained.

With the parents gone, Ava patched herself up in the bathroom with the first aid kit Lexi brought her. For the first time, Ava got a good look at her throat. A thin frost covered the five-inch slash. It astonished her to find the ice covering, she didn't remember summoning it. Ava wiped around it with a warm washcloth. It bore a crusted, bumpy texture that felt like glass. Even the washcloth could not dissolve it, but after it did snag a couple times,

Ava took greater care around the ice. She wrapped a long bandage over the wound, mainly to spare Lexi's eyes and to feel some sort of normalcy. Her clothes were in the washing machine downstairs, and Ava instead wore a periwinkle sleep shirt Lexi had loaned her.

As Ava fixed herself up, Lexi made breakfast downstairs. It wasn't much, just bacon and eggs from yesterday morning. She checked how much taro ice cream was left in the freezer and had a couple spoonfuls straight from the carton to calm her nerves.

Her phone was a mess, there were so many messages and shared news stories crowding her notifications. Even on XinBō, she couldn't get away from it. Lexi wanted her phone off and dead but she kept it close and fully charged, in case Tyrone called. *Should* Tyrone call.

What's stoppin' him from comin' in here and killin' us now? Lexi pondered as she laid down the plates. "Ava?" Lexi called up. "You doin' okay up there?"

A steady, tired gallop came down the stairs. Snow white gauze wrapped her throat, Ava sealed the end with a strip of ice as she answered, "I'm alright." The food smelled inviting, her stomach gave a light rumble. "You alright?"

Lexi finished setting the table, "...Nah. Let – let's just eat so you can ..." Lexi drifted to a pause. She looked up at Ava, folding her arms, "I wish ... why does this *have* to happen? How did you not *know* abou–"

"Ty's ... I – I don't ... I ..."

Lexi waved it off, she didn't want to start crying again.

"Forget it, forget it. Let's just ... let's just try to eat."

Breakfast was silent and quick. Neither wanted to waste time getting Ava's abilities up to speed. Ava tried to drag the pepper forward but a speeding car blasting music made her throttle it across the kitchen. When Lexi found it, the pepper case was both frozen and scorched. Thus, they moved to the living room and practiced there.

"Okay," Lexi said with a firm clap of her hands. "Can you come from there to here?"

Ava stood on the other side of the living room. It was a colorful space; large, scenic fans decorated the walls, as did beautiful portraits of meaningful Tagalog or the Harlem Renaissance. The entire house was small but filled with art, memories and love. Even the small, concrete backyard had colorful fish streamers hung on the tarnished silver fence. This was always a home of peace and fun for Ava, something she desperately wished she could feel in that moment. Instead, she nodded at Lexi and closed her eyes. She felt herself sinking down, down. The darkness enveloped her like velvet. The air laid thick but didn't suffocate. The room felt different. She opened her eyes.

Lexi staggered back, collecting inches between them. "How ... you ... Ava, you got all shadowy and went through the floor! Then you popped up again in my shadow!" Lexi exasperated, "Ty can do this, *too*? Hoooooh my god." The realization was too much, Lexi started to hyperventilate, her eyes wide with terror.

Ava collected Lexi, panic was *not* going to keep them alive. "Lex! Lex! Please, *pleeeeeeeeease*. We'll both die for *sure* if you don't help me. He'll kill me first and make you watch, you know that. *Please* help me practice. *Please*. He knows how to do this and how to do it *better*. I gotta get a hold of all this by *tonight* or we're *both* dead. Please, *please*?"

Lexi nodded, Ava could feel her shaking. Ava drew her into a tight hug.

"I don't wanna die," Ava whispered. "Please, let us practice."

Lexi nodded and thus, they resumed practice.

Over the hours, Ava became better piece by piece with Lexi's help. She threw pillows for Ava to hover or stop. She gave Ava raw meat from the freezer to shock or burn. (They also would have the cooked meats for lunch.) She provided glasses of water for Ava to freeze and then boil – a couple glasses were broken this way. Ava tried moving through her own shadow again, appearing all over the house. She even trapped Lexi's foot in a shadow through the floor for half a minute.

Even with all this practicing, Ava only felt a little ready. Compared to Tyrone's *years* of steady experience, she still felt dead in the water. Even when weaker, he still knew more. And if she didn't act soon, he wouldn't be weak for long. She didn't want to experience bloodlust either, she wanted nothing to cloud her head. It ached her heart to believe that she would have to kill her brother but no matter how she mulled over it, all roads led straight to his grave. And only she could make it so.

Ava wanted to leave before Lexi's parents returned but there was one more thing she wanted to try.

Holed away in Lexi's room, Ava asked sitting at the head of the bed, "Lexi? Can I try something?"

Lexi sat at the foot of the bed, playing a game on her phone to ease her mind. "What else is there to do?" It still creeped her out to think about her foot being trapped in a shadow. Ava sounded ... tickled when it happened. Like her brother.

"One more thing, just let me try, okay?" Ava twisted the air behind her to lace her braids together into a ponytail.

Lexi eyed Ava. "Are you gonna do something to me?"

"...Maybe?"

Lexi cringed away. "Is it gonna hurt?"

"I don't know. I don't think so. I doubt it would," Ava reasoned, mostly to herself. *Didn't seem to hurt after Ty did it.*

Hesitant, Lexi agreed and readied herself, scrunching her eyes shut and pointing her head away. "Okay, do it."

Ava closed her eyes and focused on becoming Lexi. She didn't know how she had to feel or what to concentrate on, so she started with wanting to see through Lexi's eyes.

She then opened them. Ava was staring down at Lexi's phone in her hand. It was opened to a game page in XinBō. Ava couldn't feel the phone but she could will the arm to pick it up.

"Oh my god–" Ava stopped, there was an echo. She

watched herself from Lexi's perspective, her eyes closed but her movements mimicked. As Ava spoke through Lexi, she saw her own mouth move, "Is this how Ty controls people?" She gasped, "This is how Roma and Marissa died. It was all Ty. Has he ever done this to me?"

Ava released Lexi and returned to her own vision, watching Lexi become light-headed and dizzy again.

Lexi tried to shake some sense into her head. Her voice was groggy, "Did you ... what did you *do* to me, Ava?"

Ava didn't know how to explain. "I think ... I think I can control others, like zombies."

"You *what?*"

Ava sprang from the bed. Fear thundered forth in her chest. *If I could do this and it's Ty's power ...* "I - I need to go. Ty-"

"Ava, wait!" Lexi jumped from the bed and clasped Ava's rattling wrists, "Promise me you'll come back!"

"Lex, I -"

"Promise!"

"He might kill me-"

"*Promise!*" Lexi practically shrieked, she even startled herself. She tried to recollect herself. "Promise you'll come back! No matter what happens. *Please*. Please, come back."

Ava sniffed and choked. She could feel Lexi shake. "I'll - I'll try." She smeared away any rolling tears and cleared her throat. "I'll try."

Then, Ava disappeared.

Chapter 6

The house of Tanis was dim. Evening was soon to fall. Ava landed by the couch. There, Tyrone sat, watching television. He wore a black tank and baggy cargos. The slash on his throat was cauterized shut. An old childhood cartoon played on the television. Ava recognized it, it was about the forest and magical animals. They grew up on that show, such happy memories. Cast in the dancing light laid Jermaine, still slumped over in his easy chair. The smoldering had gone, and all that remained was a stiff body and the faint after-smell of cooked flesh. Ava didn't dare look over and see her mother. Her open eyes, her twisted face. Her last moments.

Tyrone snickered at a passing commercial. He looked up at Ava, "You're a bit early, baby sister." He patted the seat beside him. "Here, sit. It's our favorite episode."

Ava sat beside him, ginger and wary. He was kind again. She leaned against him, placing her head on his shoulder. Her heart raced, she hoped he wouldn't notice. Tyrone looked down at her and smiled.

"My baby sister, she's come home," Tyrone remarked with dark joy. He pulled her chin up to look at her gauzed throat. Ava stared at the stucco ceiling as she could feel her twin brother pull away the bandages. She could feel his hot breath on her neck, the ice crystals crackled and fell away as her head was tilted back further, reopening the wound. She placed a comforting hand on the back of his head. Tyrone grew a twisted smile at his sister's acceptance. He reached down further to sop up the beading river of blood ... and she shocked him with all her might.

Tyrone erupted into a hideous roar as Ava held him close and kept sending currents and fire into him. She held her eyes tight shut as his screaming filled her head. She didn't want to see. He started to steam and convulse, but Ava didn't let up. She refused to let up until he was still and quiet. She shoved off his heavy body. It crashed into the glass top coffee table before collapsing onto the floor.

Laid among the shattered glass, the cartoon came back on, casting him in an animated glow. "What are we doin', grandpa?" pipped from the TV a childlike bird looking in a woodsy marsh beside their turtle grandfather, who sagely glanced about. Ava turned it off with a teary blink. She couldn't take her eyes off her brother's lifeless body.

The smell of fried flesh renewed in the air and hung heavy. The house was near dark, the dusky sky gave little light.

Ava didn't want to stay any longer. She got up and ran to the stairs. Ava half-expected Tyrone to stop her or appear in front of her but there he remained, laid among the shatter with a still chest and wild, frozen eyes. She was certain he was dead.

Ava felt drained climbing the stairs, almost tapped out completely. To test what little strength she had left, Ava held out a hand and tried to summon her phone through the shadows or teleportation. Through the shadows, she could feel her phone in her bookbag – and the weight of her mother's body. It was heavy and cold. Her muscles were tight, Yvonne died in absolute terror.

The phone landed in her room, bouncing onto the bed and clattered to the floor. Ava ran to her room to retrieve her phone. It was dead. Ava pocketed it and started packing. She blinked to turn on the hall light and found a drawstring bag in the mess of her room.

Nothing could keep her mind off what she had done. Over what Tyrone had done. It was difficult to see through her blurry, teary eyes but she just blinked them back as she packed like a whirlwind. Ava threw anything near her into the drawstring bag, guided more by instinct than thought.

She struggled shoving in a fat pillow when the air grew thick.

"That wasn't enough, baby sister," Tyrone tutted, slumped against her door. He opened the floor beneath her with a shadow, Ava lifted herself with an updraft. The wind was weak and faltering, so she tried to control Tyrone instead. She could feel his injury and pain but her mind erupted with slicing agony, like every nerve in her brain became alight. Ava dropped to the ground, crumpled and wincing.

Tyrone rumbled out a deep laughter. "You? Control me? My god, baby sister," Tyrone walked over to Ava, he hid his blistering pain in his slow gait. "You are being *too* adorable right now." He knelt down, "You know we can't control each other. Or else my life would have been so much easier." He laid down beside his twin, face to face. The soft cast of the hall light shone over their crowns. The stench of his roasted flesh reeked her nose.

He smiled at her sweetly as she strained and struggled against the blaring pain, "You're so lovely. Let's drink to this moment." Tyrone sat up and unsheathed the dagger from his pocket. He presented the dagger before her again, the sharpened blade glittered like stars.

No matter her effort, Ava could not send herself elsewhere, she was too tapped out. Wheezes tumbled out of her at the sight of the knife.

Tyrone reached over and picked up Ava's wrist, limp and shaking. He flipped it over to the underside and balanced the blade on her skin. Ava wrenched her eyes shut and waited for the slash. She heard a quick swipe but felt nothing. Tyrone groaned with light agony. Ava opened her eyes – Tyrone had slashed his own wrist. Blood poured down his arm like a river.

He grunted, "This is for you. Know that I'll always put

you first. But I drink first this time." With a quick snatch, he slashed her. Ava's screams filled the house. Tyrone didn't care, he drank from her wrist and drank heavily. Ava hollered and protested but she felt herself become weaker and weaker as she felt her abilities flow into her brother. It wasn't painful, she felt like water in a bucket poured out into a rapid.

Then, Tyrone laid his bloody wrist before her. She stared with deep hunger. As he drank, he watched Ava captivated by his pouring wound. She struggled towards it, he drew it away. She tried to trace after it, he smirked at her want. Power was returning to him, and never had he felt so fulfilled.

Ava had the deepest ache of hunger. She had never felt so starved. The drifting wound teased her. So desperate, she started sucking at the blood trail on the carpeted floor. This surprised Tyrone and amused him greatly. No more games, he gave his wrist to his sister, who drank slavishly. She could feel power and strength return. Ava sucked down more.

The more she drank, the more she regained. It was not long before she could sit up and hold Tyrone's wrist with her own hand. Tyrone sat up with her and did the same.

The power between them balanced out, each of them had a mix of the other's ability. Tyrone had Ava's ability of fire, ice, teleportation and telekinesis as well as his own powers and Ava added Tyrone's ability of electricity, shadow, air and control to hers. Together, they were equal. Together, they were strong.

They only stopped when the other did. Tyrone looked at his sister, her bleeding wrist nestled in his lap. She looked back with his wrist in hers. He gazed down at his sister's bloodied wrist and covered it with his hand. The air grew cold and brisk around her wrist and Tyrone lifted his hand, revealing a frost of bandage. He smiled at her and at his wrist in her lap, his mouth smeared with blood. Ava took the cue and with two delicate fingers, slid a crest of ice over his cut, tracing it shut. A heinous smile bled onto Tyrone's face. They were now the family he always imagined.

He slid his hand around Ava and laid her back across his folded lap. Tyrone stroked Ava's head with love and care. Ava's eyes danced about, studying his face. It was calm and content, he looked down upon her with steady, adoring eyes.

"Baby sister," he spoke softly, "we're one, now."

Ava smiled back, "We are, big brother."

Tyrone exhaled a tired sigh. His breath smelled of iron. "Let us rest together. The world can wait for us."

Ava nodded, her smile never fading. She played along, she needed more time. She needed rest.

In an instant, they both laid on Tyrone's bed. Tyrone plucked his tablet from under Ava's legs.

"Can't crush that," he warned. "That's our bible. All of who we are rests *here*." He placed the tablet on a short table of ice sprouted from his bed knob.

Ava laid against the wall and Tyrone laid beside her. The comforter underneath them appeared above them and drifted down delicately with a sheet of air. Tyrone nuzzled her head and slipped a comforting hand on her waist. He rubbed it as he drifted off to sleep.

Ava felt soft butterfly kisses over her face from the wind as she watched him fall into slumber. He sometimes ran his hand over the entirety of her side. She tried not to flinch.

I can't die like this, Ava resolved as she drifted off herself.

Ava's eyes shot open two hours later. It was the middle of the night. The hallway light was off, the moon gave the only light. Tyrone still faced her, dead asleep and mouth crusted with blood, just like hers. She watched her brother, scared he'd wake up next. He was completely out, his hand draped over her waist.

The rest did her some good. Ava wasn't whole but she was better. An idea had come to mind.

Slow and gentle, Ava folded her arm to herself. She didn't dare want to wake him. It took little muster for a long, icy blade to extend from the side of her fist. Its arc glinted in the moonlight as she propped herself up, bit by bit. Looking down upon her slumbering brother, Ava steeled her nerves. She still didn't want to but there was no other way.

In one swift swipe, Ava slashed Tyrone's throat deep and wide. Tyrone woke up grasping at his throat and rasping for air as Ava scrambled out of the bed. She darted into the dark hall, covered in a spray of his blood.

Then, she stopped, cloaked in the hall's darkness. She remembered the last time what good running away did her. She had to be sure he was dead this time. And powerless.

Ava returned to the room. There, Tyrone writhed, flooding out. Squelches of blood squeaked out from the soaked mattress as he tried to freeze his wound shut. Too much blood had poured out and he couldn't breathe, his windpipe was cleanly severed. He gaped and gasped but couldn't draw in any air. He looked about wildly until his eyes focused on Ava propping herself above him. He motioned for her to close his throat with desperate clutches.

Ava dropped down and drank from his throat. Blood streamed like a fountain as she held his forehead still against the pillow. Tyrone tried to shock or burn her but it was useless, he already had lost too much. He tried to pry her off but his fingers were slick and weak. Tyrone was helpless, he felt emptied like a bucket into an ocean. The cold started to reach him, the room darkened. He listened to her hungry feeding drift further and further away until he couldn't see her at all. His dear little sister.

Scared and weakened, Tyrone slipped away.

It was over. No more resistance met Ava. New strength surged through her veins. More power. She lifted her head, half her face soaked. Her brother's eyes held so much terror and sorrow. With a gentle hand, she closed them.

She had finally killed her own brother.

Ava choked out a sob and mourned. She laid her head upon his chest and held his chilly hands. She mourned for whatever good buried far too deep inside him she had extinguished. She mourned for her mother. She mourned for her father. She mourned for how they died and that she watched them die, doing nothing. She mourned for all their futures cut short. She mourned for what she had to do. She mourned for herself.

She wailed, she cried. She wished for time to turn back, for a different way, for a different life. Now, she was alone, orphaned by her own hand and her brother's.

There, she stayed and mourned.

Chapter 7

Morning had come. Lexi sat on the edge of her bed, waiting. Her 7:30 alarm rang and still no Ava. Her eyes misted over as she checked her phone for the umpteenth time. No sign of her, just emails and inane messages. Her social media was starting to look a little normal, there was less chatter about what happened. Byron checked in on Lexi after Ava left, but Lexi ignored his text.

Lexi wanted a signal, anything. She feared calling, what if Ava was hiding and had to stay silent? What if Tyrone picked up instead? *What if she was dead?*

Lexi's whined into a creeping cry. Her fallen tears magnified drops of her screen. She wiped the screen dry with her shirt. She had to know, she had to. Lexi called Ava.

The phone rang. And rang. And rang. Then a cheerful recording played, "This is Ava. Leave me a message!" Lexi hung up.

She's dead.

Lexi wailed into her pillow. She knew it. Ava was gone. Lexi was an only child; Ava felt like a sister to her. And now, she was alone again.

A hand rubbed her back, comforting her. Lexi bawled harder into her pillow.

"Mamaaaaaaaaa," Lexi cried, smearing her wet face against the pillow, "Ava *died*! She died, Mama!" She broke down again, her body rattled with heavy sobs, "I couldn't even *do* nothin'!"

"Lex, I'm right here," Ava sniffed. "I – I said I'd come back," she quivered with a faint smile.

Lexi whipped around and cleared her eyes. There Ava stood before her, cleaned up and with a bloated bag hung over her shoulder. Clean gauze covered her throat and wrist, all sealed with a glinting, thin piece of ice. She had on a baggy shirt and baggier pants, the pockets filled with whatever she couldn't get into her bag.

Overjoyed, Lexi rocketed off the bed and wrapped her arms around Ava, "You're ... you're here! Wait ..." she parted from Ava, " ... does ... does ... what happened to ..."

"He's ... he's gone," Ava couldn't hold it in much longer, her face crumpled up as she slumped into Lexi's shoulder.

Astonished by the news, Lexi stroked Ava's head. She tried to console her but her words faltered, "He ... he was...

Ava, you knew how Ty was. And with *powers*? There's no way he wouldn't hav-"

Shannon poked her head in, her royal blue satin bonnet tied up and she herself barely awake, "Baby girl, you called me? ... Ava?"

Lexi wasted no time to answer. "Ma! Ava stayed the night because her brother went off. I snuck her in after y'all slept. Look!" She turned Ava around and tried to show her wounds. Ava wouldn't have any of it, she knelt her head and folded her arms. Lexi urged, "C'mon, Ava! Show her! She–"

"I – I believe," Shannon halted with an upheld hand, much more awake now. "I believe. Ava, did your brother really hurt you?" She knew from her daughter that Tyrone had a time-bomb temper but never did she believe it would become this bad. Ava always tried to cover for her brother when Lexi bad-mouthed him.

Ava sank down on the bed and curled up in tears. Her wrist and neck stung from her hard crying. She tried to pull up a sleeve to cover her bandaged wrist but it snapped back, too short. The sight of the bandage disturbed Shannon, she silently urged her daughter forth and stepped out the room.

"What *happened* to her?" Shannon asked in a quick whisper. "Will she need a rape kit?"

Lexi shook her head and hugged her mother. "She stopped him before that. But ...," Lexi trailed off into tears.

Phillip tightened his mauve robe as he ambled down the hall, "Is Lexi crying?" He patted and stroked his daughter's head. He heard another whine of mourning from inside her room. "Is someon–"

Shannon shushed him with a finger to her lips. "Ava," she mouthed. "Her brother tried to rape her."

Phillip's jaw dropped. He whisked into Lexi's room and found Ava deep in sorrow. He dropped to his knees to look at her hidden face. Ava turned away. Never had Phillip met Tyrone but outside of Ava, he had never heard good things about him either. Softly, he reached out and asked, "Hey, Ava? Ava? It's Mr. Dimaanó, you're safe here. You can be here as *long* as you like, as long as you like." Ava kept avoiding his gaze, the sight broke his heart. "Hey, hey, I'm – I'm going to try to make it okay. But I'm going to need your help to make it oka–"

"I killed my brother!" Ava flooded out. "I can't believe I killed my brother!"

The outburst allowed Phillip to witness Ava's bandages. Her wrist bandage came loose and he saw a fraction of the slash as Ava re-wrapped it. The sight sickened him. He looked up at his family. They watched Ava with helpless pity.

The police came. One squad car parked at the Dimaanós', four at the Tanis'. Ava sat on the Dimaanós' couch in the living room between Lexi and Shannon. Phillip stood beside the officer standing in their living room, hearing the cold confirmation crackle from the radio: three bodies, two adults, one minor. No matter how much Phillip pressed, Ava refused all test kits. She just wanted everything behind her.

The officer was cold and direct, there only to do his job and leave. He gave an endless barrage of questions: When did this happen? (Last night) How did this happen? (Tyrone killed them) *Exactly*, how did this happen? (I don't know) With what? (I don't know) What did he try to do to you? (Cut my throat and wrist?) With what? (A knife) From where? (I don't know) Was he always like this, has Tyrone ever hit you before? (No) Was he violent to his parents, his mother, his father? (No – sometimes – no, no, he didn't) Are you sure? Has he ever abused you? (...Please don't make me answer that) Has he ever abused you? (Please ... a different question) Are you the only surviving victim? (Yes) Do you have anyone you can stay with? (Yes) How long has Tyrone acted this way? (All our lives?) Has he tried to kill before? (No) What started this? (An argument with Dad) Were you there when any of them died–

"Ava? Ava, you're staring off again," said Lexi. Her plate of mashed potatoes and turkey was almost empty. Ava's had gone cold. "You want Ma or I to reheat your plate?"

Ava was still and silent. Her gaze was far away, staring at her plate.

It was dinnertime. The police had long gone, as had the bodies. Ava's home was a crime scene, though. That didn't bother Ava, she was quite numb by now.

Shannon sat next to Lexi. She had watched Ava the whole time, just like Phillip next to Ava.

He tried to console with a gentle tone, "Things are going to ... they're going to be alright, ok? You got us. Lexi has an amazing best friend and we're going to love her with all we got." The details that poured out of Ava, the wounds she showed, it infuriated him that no one picked up on Tyrone's behavior sooner. Including himself. He couldn't help but sit beside Ava and watch her with sorry eyes.

Ava was still and silent. Her distant gaze remained unmoved.

Lexi picked up Ava's limp hand and held it in her lap. Still no response. The Dimaanós exchanged uncertain looks with each other. This had never been Ava. She was now a simple shell.

Shannon repeated her husband, a little firmer. "Ava, no more harm will come to you. It's all over now."

Still and silent. Ava blinked slowly.

Shannon shifted in her seat and asked, "Ava? Can you look at Lexi or me?"

Ava lifted her head up, eyes dead. The day wouldn't stop playing again and again in her head. Her brother bleeding out. Her father's body illuminated by the TV. The questioning. Her mother's scream. *Ava. Pretty little Ava–*

Phillip shook Ava's shoulder, she jumped out her chair and scurried back on the floor, "Ty, *stop!*" Her breath collected a terrible wheeze that subsided as she scanned the room. Everyone was up at the table. A floating iron pan in the kitchen hooked itself back onto the wall.

Ava broke down into a thunderous cry.

Epilogue

Oct 23, 2013

TwipView: Private

Subject: Doesn't get it

Ava is so stupid. She has no idea about herself and refuses to listen to me. We're capable of so much. All this different kinds of psychokinesis and she's wasting it. One day, she'll come around. She has to. Ive been working on my side for years, it will be a pain bringing her up to speed but I'm her brother. I gotta do it.

> Ma and dad need to stop brainwashing her
> about me, tho. They don't know ANYTHING
> about us. They gave birth to GODS and want
> us to live as dumb mortals. At first I believed
> this but the more I read, the more I
> understood. Bab.Sis. and I, we're more than
> this. We're the new world.
>
> The new world
>
> They're gonna be gone if they don't watch
> themselves. Everybody who stands in our
> way. She is the Beginning. I am the End.
>
> One day the fun will begin.

Ava darkened the tablet and rubbed her eyes. Spring Break had arrived and Ava sat in her room as Lexi packed her overloaded suitcase downstairs. A family trip was coming up and Phillip and Shannon were out buying last minute vacation needs. Ava had been living with the Dimaanós since the incident; they gave her the guest bedroom upstairs, close to Lexi's room. Phillip and Shannon took care of the paperwork that came Ava's way – and they were lucky both Yvonne and Jermaine had insurance, which gave Ava the house, but it didn't make anything easier. There were no funerals, just a single memorial service. Yvonne and Jermaine shared a beautiful red urn together that sat atop Ava's particle wood dresser. Tyrone's ashes sat in a small white box hidden away at the bottom of the dresser, far in the back. The Dimaanós never knew, they thought Tyrone's remains were discarded, at Ava's request. She made them think that way. Ava never wanted to throw her brother away, just avoid discord. She couldn't bring herself to do it.

No one knew Ava kept Tyrone's tablet, either. She nabbed it through the shadows before it could be discovered. There laid all of Tyrone in digital form: his private Twip Journal, his notes, the sites he visited, everything. Occasionally, Ava came across family pictures but those were quite rare. The tablet was all about him. And Ava. How they could grow, how they could function. How they could destroy. Together and in lockstep – with Tyrone at the helm.

The police didn't meddle much, Ava made sure of it. She controlled whoever she had to, to bury whatever curiosity anyone had. Soon enough, Ava received a report that stated what occurred in a simple, frank manner: Tyrone Tanis had an argument with his dad while the whole family was having dinner. He snapped, killed dad, killed mom – signs point to taser use – tried to slash Ava apart with a kitchen knife. Ava got control of the knife and killed in self-defense. Open-and-shut case.

Ava got the Tanis' house as heir and the insurance paid the rest of it off. She had yet to set foot back in that place. Crime scene cleaners took care of most of the carnage and damage but still she didn't want to return. Though, without knowing, some nights she returned to her old bed as she slept, teleporting back as she stirred awake.

Returning to school was just as difficult. The principal sent out a letter:

> It is with heavy hearts here at Melissa Elliot H.S. #28 today to say we have lost another one of our own and in such a short time. Tyrone Tanis, Sophomore, pursued Literature and History. Creative and bright, Tyrone spoke his mind and never gave up.
>
> There is nothing to be said, short of horrific, of the circumstances surrounding his parents' passing. They are survived by Ava Tanis, Sophomore. We surround her with love and appreciation, so she may see some light in this dark time.
>
> We, the administration, would like to remind students that grievance counselors are available. Tyrone will be dearly missed.

Ava kept her head low and tried to focus on her studies. She declined all counseling, she'd rather speak to no one. The whispers still followed her, but at least they weren't as cruel as before. The teachers went easier on her. Ava made them.

"Avaaaaaaaa!" Lexi called as she dashed up the stairs. "Ava, d'you think I should bring th– Ava?"

Ava sat on her bed, still. She had stumbled upon a picture in the tablet, one she forgot existed. It was a selfie

Tyrone had taken with her when he first got the tablet. They were in a store, standing in front of a silly snowman. Smiling and happy. Tyrone's head towered above Ava's with a ridiculous face, Ava couldn't hold in her laughter as she peered up at him. *Little Ava. Pretty little Ava–*

"Is that Tyrone's?" Lexi took a closer look, "Is it?"

Quietly, Ava replied, "It is."

Lexi sucked in an angered breath. "Give it here, Ava," she demanded, "It's gonna mess with your head!"

Ava stayed still. The air grew a touch brisk.

"Now!"

Ava sank into tears, "He's the only one who knew who I truly was–"

"He *twisted* your head!" Lexi shot back. "He tried to *kill* you! Why can't you *see* that–"

"You think I can't?" Ava snapped. A strong breeze rushed through the room, and Lexi took a step back. Ava floated off the bed, "You think I can't?"

"A-Ava, try to calm down," Lexi tried to stand her ground but the cutting cold gale made it difficult. Lexi could hardly open her eyes, "Ava, *please!*"

The gale stopped.

"I don't know *how* to feel," Ava sniffed. "I ... can't. I can't think *straight*." Her breath tattered, she touched the healing scar on her neck, "I hide who I am from everyon–"

"Not me!" Lexi corrected.

Ava drew up a ball of fire in her hand. Mesmerized by the brilliance, she asked, "Would your parents keep me if they knew what I could do –"

"We're gonna tell 'em this week!" Lexi reminded, "We talked about this, Ava." Ava's tone and how she gazed at the flame concerned Lexi. "*Please* give me the tablet. You deserve a new life!"

Ava doused the fire and looked at the tablet. She sank it into a plate of shadow. "I don't know what I deserve." Her baleful eyes looked upon Lexi's horrified face, "I'm sorry, Lex."

"Why–" Lexi became still and slouched. Ava was much better at controlling others now.

Ava rubbed her face dry the best she could. "I am so, so sorry, Lexi. I'm still figurin' this out myself. He's in my dreams. He's in my nightmares. He *is* my nightmares. But I still don't know how to feel yet. I just ... I need *time*. I need time. And I need you to forget."

Lexi resumed, back to her normal self. "Hey, Ava!" she bubbled with delight, "D'you think I should bring the Macau towel or the grapevine one?"

Ava answered, "Grapevine."

Lexi's face brightened, "I thought so, too!" She clapped her hands, a thought struck her, "Oh! And we're gonna show Ma and Dad what you can do, nice and slow, okay? Maybe snowballs or marshmallows or somethin'?" Lexi couldn't wait, they had been planning for weeks.

Ava cracked a small smile, "Let's warm them up with marshmallows."

Other works

Null(Void)

In Search of Amika

Dreamer

About the Author

MultiMind lives in Baltimore, Maryland. She tries to find time for her countless hobbies, from 3D printing to bookbinding to virtual reality. She writes books that are fairly Black, quite queer, and very much embedded in the world of Sci-Fi, Fantasy & Horror.

MULTIMIND Publishing